Death in Unlikely Places

A Max Hurlock Roaring 20s Mystery

By John Reisinger

www.johnreisinger.com
Glyphworks Publishing
2014

Glyphworks Publishing
2014
Death in Unlikely Places
A Max Hurlock Roaring 20s Mystery

Copyright 2014 by John Reisinger
www.johnreisinger.com

Glyphworks Publishing, 2014

Acknowledgements

As with any book, a great many people contributed their time and specialized knowledge to help produce the final product. I wish to thank the following and apologize to anyone I may have left out.

The St Augustine Historical Society
The Villa Zorayda, St Augustine
The Davis Shores Home Owners Association, St Augustine

And of course, my wife Barbara, who helps make it all come together.

John Reisinger

A killer who strikes again and again, and whose every crime is impossible

In 1926, a letter from a world famous aviator launches Max Hurlock on the most complex and diabolical case of his career. Max and Allison travel to Florida, where a serial killer is on the loose, a serial killer whose every crime is seemingly impossible!

A man is stabbed to death in a small locked room apparently while shooting at his killer.

A man goes fishing on an almost empty lake in full view of a marina, and is found bludgeoned to death.

A man gets on an empty elevator on the first floor and arrives on the fourth floor shot to death.

A man is found shot to death and his body draped over a tree limb 20 feet in the air.

A man is seen entering his private art gallery by numerous witnesses, but is found alone and shot twice behind a locked door a few minutes later.

The newspapers are calling the killer The Invisible Man. Who is committing these crimes, and how is he doing them? Max and Allison must race the clock to stop a man who seems to be part killer and part magician.

Cast of Characters

Maryland
Max and Allison Hurlock
Isis Dalrymple-town librarian
Chip Carswell-local newspaper editor
Bubba Henderson-schoolmate of Max's

Florida
Roy G. Atley-St John's County Sheriff
Julian DeKuyper-St Augustine gadabout
Nancy-new Davis Shores homeowner

The Victims
Thomas Russo- Jacksonville
Robert Godfrey-Lake George
Jerome Daniels-Orlando
Henry LaPointe-Marion
Calvin Warfield-Melbourne

The Suspects
Sean McGuiness
Ronald Anderson
Mario Carpellini
Ryan Summers

Historical figures
Glenn Curtiss
Lena Curtiss
James Bright
D.P. Davis

Chapter 1
Death in a private place

Everyone was surprised at just how much blood a thick wool sweater could absorb.

Just south of Jacksonville, Florida, the body of Tom Russo was slumped in the leather chair at his desk in his locked private office. He was a middle-aged, balding man, and looked surprisingly peaceful. Although he had a pistol next to his hand and a hole in his blood-soaked sweater, not a drop of blood had reached the floor. There were several dried red streaks on the desk and on the pistol, but otherwise, all the blood was in the sweater.

The office was small, and smelled slightly of the old dark paneling and an oriental rug. On a wall next to the desk was an art deco poster of a shapely woman waterskiing behind a mahogany Chris Craft. On the bottom of the poster was simply the word "Florida".

St John's County Sheriff Roy G. Atley and two deputies had responded to the frantic call and now stood in front of the desk frowning.

"Anybody find a suicide note?" asked the sheriff. The deputies shook their heads.

"There was no note anywhere, sheriff," said a secretary, obviously very flustered. "That's just the way I found him this morning. I have the only other key to the office, you see, so I unlock it in the morning if Mr. Russo isn't in. This morning, the door was locked, so I unlocked it just the way I always do, and...well, I found him like this."

"Has anyone notified his wife?"

"Yes. She's on her way here."

"Could you show me your key?"

Atley looked at the key she was holding and nodded. "That matches the key we found in the door on the inside, so both keys are accounted for. Body's cold, so it must have happened last night. Did he usually work alone at night...and on Sundays?"

"All the time. He said it was quiet and he could think better."

"Looks like he was maybe thinking he was tired of living," Atley muttered, looking under the desk. "What does, er what *did* Russo do, anyway?"

"This is Russo properties. Mr. Russo was a property developer here in Florida. He'd buy and sell everything from lots to houses."

"Did he usually wear a heavy sweater?"

"Not during the week, but it was pretty cool yesterday and he was alone. He hated to turn the heat on. He'd always say 'This is Florida! Why am I paying for heat?'."

"Uh huh. Do you know any reason he'd want to end it all? Was he depressed or anything?"

The secretary sighed, but shook her head.

"Where is he?" came another female voice. "Let me in. I'm his wife. Oh, my God!"

The woman who entered the room stood frozen near the desk and the grisly scene. Sheriff Atley turned to her.

"I'm sorry, Mrs. Russo. I'm Sheriff Atley. Do you feel well enough to help us out by answering a few questions?"

She looked dazed, then turned to Atley.

"Wha..what sort of questions?"

"Was your husband depressed or suicidal lately?"

"I don't know. Look, could we talk about this someplace else?"

"Of course. I know this is terrible for you."

A few minutes later, Atley was sitting with the wife in a conference room over cups of coffee.

"Business was turning lousy," she said suddenly.

Atley nodded both sympathy and encouragement.

"Tom was a developer. He'd buy up tracts of land and subdivide it into building lots for sale. For the last few years, he made so much money we didn't know where to stash it all. People were buying land sight unseen and using up their savings to do it. Ever since the war, more people have bought cars and roads have gotten better, so people have been coming to Florida to vacation and get away in the winter. Pretty soon a lot of these vacationers wanted a piece of Florida to call their own, so Tom and others started buying up property and subdividing it, then selling the building lots. People snapped them up like hotcakes."

"And they were building on it?" Atley asked.

She shrugged. "A few were, and some held the land to build on when they retired, but the demand was so great that it drove up prices until many people started buying just to resell, sometimes in the same day. It was crazy. A lot of people made a lot of dough selling and reselling all over Florida, but then it started to come apart."

"How's that?" said Atley.

"Things have started to cool down. The buyers weren't coming as fast and people were having trouble reselling. And what's worse, they were having trouble making the payments. Tom told me that half the people he sold land to were behind in their payments. Some of them were starting to blame him for the lousy market. So, yeah, I guess he was depressed, or at least

3

worried. But I never thought he'd do anything like this."

A deputy stuck his head in the door.

"The coroner's people are here to take the body away. Are you ready to release it yet?"

"Have we got photographs?"

"Just finishing up now."

"All right. Unless the autopsy turns up something startling. It looks like a suicide brought on by the pressure of business. I'm sorry, Mrs. Russo."

Mrs. Russo daubed her eyes and looked up.

"So it was definitely a suicide, sheriff?"

Atley took a sip of coffee. "Well, he was apparently killed by a self-inflicted gunshot wound while in his locked office with the gun by his hand, so that lets out anyone else. Besides, the business problems certainly give him a motive. I don't know what else it could be."

She sat slowly shaking her head. "I just never thought he would ever do anything like this. Never."

Atley nodded in sympathy.

"I guess you just never can tell."

Sheriff Roy G. Atley stepped back out on to the street, lit a cigarette and exhaled slowly. The sun was shining and a nearby palm tree rustled in the breeze; another beautiful Florida day. He shook his head.

"What the hell gets into people?" he said.

A few days later, the Jacksonville District Attorney called Sheriff Atley.

"Morning, Roy G. I just got the autopsy on that Tom Russo suicide. I'm looking through it now."

"Any surprises?"

The DA thumbed through the pages. "Doesn't look like it. Time of death matches up, powder residue on his hand from firing the gun, one shot was fired..."

"Pretty much what I expected," said Atley. "We already determined that the gun had been recently fired."

The DA mumbled as he read, then suddenly stopped.

"What the hell?"

"What's the matter? Something doesn't fit?"

The DA made a low groan. "Yeah, you might say that."

"Well?"

"Tom Russo wasn't shot, and no bullet was found."

"Not shot? But the gun *had* been fired. And Russo was definitely dead. How..."

"It seems our friend Mr. Russo was stabbed to death!"

If Atley had been smoking a cigarette, he would surely have swallowed it at that moment. "Stabbed to death? You mean with a knife?"

"You know some other way of stabbing a guy? A hatpin maybe?"

"Stabbed. Are they sure?"

"There's no doubt," said the District Attorney. "A knife wound is pretty distinctive. Your boys probably missed it at first because of the sweater."

"Well, then where was the bullet? The gun had been fired and there was no bullet found in the office. The slug had to go somewhere."

"How would I know? Maybe Russo fired it at the killer and missed."

"In that office? Impossible. There's no place in it that's more than ten feet from where Russo was sitting. He couldn't have missed. So where's the killer's body, or at least his blood?" Atley sputtered.

The District Attorney tossed the autopsy report on his desk. "Son of a...Just when I thought we had a clean case here. Looks like you have some more investigating to do, Roy G.. Now we need to find a killer, it seems. What's more, we need to know how the killer got into a small locked office, somehow stabbed a man while the victim was apparently firing at him from just a few feet away, avoided being killed himself, and then disappeared from the locked office without a key and without a trace."

Chapter 2
Mussolini and the dogsleds

Several weeks later and almost 800 miles away from the puzzling events in Jacksonville, Max and Allison Hurlock sat at a small table in Bemis's General Store eating sandwiches prepared by Betty Bemis. Betty was justly famous for her sandwiches and had recently put in a few small tables to cope with the demand. It was a cold winter's day in early March and Max and Allison had gone to St Michaels as a way to get out of the house for a while. The sandwiches were a welcome change from Allison's cooking as well.

"Pretty cold today. eh folks?" said Bill Bemis, who had something of a talent for stating the obvious. "I'd sure hate to be tonging for oysters out there today. I've seen men come back with ice in their hair and blue fingers. That's if they manage to come back at all. That's a tough business, and it's tougher when it's this cold out."

"Cold is right. Looks like snow tonight," Max replied. "We've put in some extra firewood."

"I hear some folks are heading to Florida," Bemis continued. "I hear folks sleep in tents just to enjoy the warmer weather. Lordy, what a world."

He walked away shaking his head.

"What a world indeed," Allison agreed. She had been thumbing through the newspaper. "That bag of wind Mussolini keeps grabbing dictatorial powers for himself in Italy. Those blockhead National Socialists in Germany are probably green with envy. Why is it that the people who can't properly run their own lives are the ones most anxious to run everyone else's?"

She picked up the front page, then threw it down again.

"Remember about this time last year, Max? They had that terrible Diphtheria epidemic up in Alaska."

"Nome."

"Right. They organized dogsledders to get the Diphtheria serum to Nome. There was no other way to get the serum there and people were dying. It took the volunteers five days through storms and temperatures of sixty below, but they stopped the epidemic in its tracks. It was thrilling. It made you proud."

Max nodded. "And the dogsledders were all volunteers. Imagine; all those people risking their lives to save others. Maybe there's hope for the world after all."

Allison sighed and put the paper down. "Unfortunately the dogsledders aren't the ones running things. Too often, the Mussolinis are in charge."

Max looked at her. "Allison, I know the weather's bad, and the world is in its usual turmoil, but I have a feeling that's not what's really eating you."

"Oh, it's nothing really. I'm fine. I guess it's just the winter weather."

"Don't ever go into politics, Allison. You have absolutely no talent for lying. Now spill it; what's going on?"

She was silent for a few seconds, then replied.

"Max, we've been married for over six years now. We've been a lot of places and had some great times."

"And I'm more in love with you than the day we met," said Max.

She smiled faintly. "Oh, it's been wonderful, but Max, do you ever think it's time for us to..."

"To what?"

"To start a family?"

"You mean kids?"

"That's usually how it's done."

Max took her hand and grinned.

"As long as they look like you, count me in."

"I'll promise you one thing," said Allison, with a determined look on her face. "Our child will be a dogsled driver-not a Mussolini."

"Great," said Max, with rising enthusiasm. "To tell you the truth, I've been thinking about it myself. All these cases I've been dragged into and all the articles you've written are exciting enough, but I think a little domestic tranquility would be just the thing."

Allison perked up so much she seemed to sparkle. "Oh, Max, it'll be wonderful. We can fix the guest bedroom up into a nursery. Your mother can knit a blanket and mine can shop for nursery rhyme books. Our fathers can take turns bragging."

Max looked thoughtful. "Hmmm. If you thought they were eccentric before, just wait until they're grandparents."

"It might be entertaining at that. Anyway, I can still write my articles and even start that novel I've been thinking about. I can work on it while the baby is sleeping."

"Uhhh. I'm not an expert on things maternal," said Max, "but I've never heard anyone say the words 'baby' and 'free time' in the same sentence without adding the word 'none'."

"Well, we'll just have to see, I suppose," said Allison. "Anyway, it'll be worth it when little Max junior starts running around annoying the ducks."

"You bet," said Max.

"Well, I have to say, I'm pleasantly surprised that you are so receptive to the idea," said Allison.

"Of course. Why not?"

"Well, a while ago I asked you what you thought of kids and you said they were like adults only without the restraint."

"Oh, not *our* kids. They'll be too busy delivering serum to Alaska or tying tin cans to Mussolini. Besides, in order to have children, I am selflessly ready to do my duty, and the sooner the better."

"I take it you're ready to return home?"

"My home fires are already burning."

An hour later, they lay in bed under several quilts. The room was cold since Max hadn't taken the time to stoke the fire when they got home.

"Well, I'm certainly enjoying parenting so far," said Max contentedly.

"Let me know how much you enjoy getting out of bed and stirring up the fire," said Allison.

"Give me a few more minutes."

Max finally got out of bed, threw on a robe, and put some more wood on the fire. He dove back under the covers shivering.

"One thing's for sure; I'll never be driving a dog team."

"We all have our talents, I suppose. Some are dogsled drivers and a few are Mussolinis."

Max stretched contentedly. "Yes; everybody's different, but not as much as you might think sometimes. It's like old Bubba Henderson back in school."

"Not more rustic reminiscences."

10

"Now Bubba," said Max, warming to his subject, "was the class clown, but he wasn't trying to be. He was always the one who fell off the swing, or dropped his lunch in the road or got caught napping in class. He had a good heart, and he'd do anything for you, but you didn't want him to because he'd foul it up."

"You certainly had some interesting friends. So I suppose he's a tycoon of some sort now."

"I don't know what he's doing. I heard he lives in Annapolis."

"Too bad. I was sort of hoping there'd be a point to the story."

"Ah, but there is; a hidden lesson to the tale."

"Very well hidden so far," Allison observed.

"Once, in fifth grade, the teacher decided that poor old Bubba needed some responsibility to straighten him out, so she appointed him official hall monitor and waited for him to rise to the occasion."

"And did he?"

"Well, a strange thing happened. At first, Bubba was the most conscientious hall monitor you ever saw. He kept detailed records of who was out of class, who was disruptive, and how many kids were late for class. The teacher loved it and was patting herself on the back."

"I can sense a 'however' coming up," said Allison.

"Right. The problem was that the power started to go to his head. He became the hall dictator, yelling at people and threatening to place them on report. He even brought in a whistle one day and started demanding hall passes. Well, pretty soon, he became the only hall monitor to be impeached."

"Power corrupts."

"And that's the point. If power can make a guy like Bubba Henderson into a monster, it's too dangerous to

11

give out in large doses. Bubba started out as a dogsled driver and wound up as Mussolini."

Allison nodded. "It sounds like Betty Pringle at Eastern High School. She was Miss Congeniality until they put her on the yearbook committee. Then she became a drill sergeant. So did Bubba come back down to earth once he was deposed?"

"Yes, but sometimes you'd see him in the hall just looking around with a wistful look in his eye."

Allison smiled and didn't reply. Since it was still cold in the house, she decided talk about something else.

"Say Max, did you ever think about going to Florida?"

"Geez, I'm not *that* cold."

"Oh, I don't mean just for the warmth; I mean to see what it's all about. People have been going crazy down there buying property, setting up trailer parks, sleeping in tents."

"So I've heard. What made you think of Florida; the cold weather?"

"Not really. I've been thinking of writing an article about it. I think I could sell it to several magazines. I've put out some feelers and gotten some interest, but no one is willing to pay to send me down there."

"So write a more general article to generate interest and then ask for an advance to do an in depth follow up."

"Hmmm. That might work. We'll see. Oh, by the way, who was that pal of yours who does all the decoy carving?"

"You mean Knobby Miller down in Whitman?"

"That's the one. Does he do work on request?"

"You want a decoy carved?"

"Not a decoy, but a wood carving of a bird."

"Sure. Old Knobby'll carve a statue of your grandmother if you'll give him a couple of dollars. As for a bird, why by the time he gets finished, you'll swear the thing could fly. I'll give you his address."

The next day, while Max worked on some things around the house, Allison went in to Whitman to look up Knobby Miller, then to St Michaels to see Isis Dalrymple at the library. Isis made it a point to know almost everything about almost everything.

"Florida?" she said. "Oh, I can tell you all about Florida. I have an aunt who lives in Sarasota. That's on the Gulf Coast. She says the place is crazy with tourists, homesteaders, and so called real estate investors. Some days she can hardly walk out to her mailbox without some northern jasper in a Model T offering to buy her place."

"I'd like to talk to her," said Allison. "It sounds like she has the inside story of the real estate boom down there."

Isis Dalrymple nodded.

"I'll give you her name and address, but you can find out plenty closer to home. Newton Wilson over towards Claiborne bought some property down there and he's mad as a wet hen about it."

"Mad?"

"Yeah. He read about how the property is making people rich, so he thought he'd get in on it. Well, a few months ago, he bought a lot south of St Augustine. He held on to it for about a month, then figured he'd waited long enough, so he went to sell it for a fat profit."

"After a month? That's a little soon, isn't it?"

"Allison, my aunt tells me some people have sold property for a big profit the same day they bought it!

That's how crazy it is down there. People are fighting for property. They buy it from newspaper ads sight unseen."

"It sounds like the Dutch Tulip Mania I once read about."

"Exactly," said Isis, thrilled that someone else in town was almost as well read as she was. "In the 1600s in Holland, the wealthy went crazy over rare tulip bulbs and bid up the prices to ridiculous levels."

"But didn't the Tulip market suddenly collapse?"

Isis nodded. "You bet it did, and a lot of rich Dutchmen suddenly became poor. They bet on prices going up forever, and they didn't. And that's just what's happening in Florida today. Newton Wilson didn't even break even! He couldn't find a buyer. Then he got behind in his payments. Well, that's no surprise. He never expected to hold the property long enough to make more than one or two payments anyway. The bank foreclosed and now Newton has no land and very little left of his life savings."

"Is this going on everywhere in Florida?"

"Not everywhere yet. Some of the more solid developments are holding on, but the chain reaction is spreading. Mark my words, Allison, there will be a lot of very unhappy people before this is over."

Chapter 3
Preparations

The same time Allison was talking about Florida with Isis Dalrymple, a medium height man in a floppy hat knocked at the door of a rundown shack just south of St Augustine, Florida. A few seconds later, a woman appeared in a faded housedress, wiping her hands on a dishtowel. She peered at him through a torn screen door.

"Yes?"

"Good morning. I'm here about your ad in the Jacksonville Times."

The woman looked blank for a second, then called to her husband. "Carl. There's a man here about the ad."

Carl appeared with a newspaper in his hand. He was short, pudgy and balding. He squinted at the newcomer. The man at the door was wearing dark glasses and had a mustache that mostly covered his mouth. Carl started for a second, then nodded.

"How ya doing? You came about the..."

"That's right."

"It's out back. Come on. I'll show you. You from around here, Mister?"

The stranger made no reply.

"I figured what with all the out of state vacation people around, I could make a quick sale," Carl continued. "Of course, it's a little tougher since I haven't got me one of those telephones yet. I figure there's not that many people I'm all that anxious to talk to."

The stranger still said nothing.

"Well, here we are."

The back yard was a tangle of weeds and various boats, automobiles and nondescript pieces of rusting farm equipment. A sleeping brown dog raised his shaggy head a moment, then flopped down again. The humming of insects rose and fell.

"It's right over here."

The stranger nodded, then walked around inspecting the item while Carl looked on anxiously.

"This looks like canvas."

"That's right," said Carl. "That makes it a lot lighter. Lift it up and you'll see. I mean, it ain't much to look at, but there's a lot of life left in it if you're careful."

The man nodded, but didn't reply.

"I don't get out as much as I used to," said Carl. "I hurt my leg and, well, you know..."

"How much?"

"Uh, well, I'm asking $20, but I'd be willing to negotiate some..."

"Twenty will be fine," said the man, taking out a roll of bills and counting off the amount. I'll take it with me. You can help me load it on my automobile."

"Oh...well, fine. You won't be sorry, mister."

The man nodded.

"I'm sure I won't be."

Chapter 4
Where's Bubba?

The next day was cold and overcast in St Michaels. Max and Allison drove up to Easton to delve into newspaper files of the Star-Democrat and to stop by the Easton library in hopes of finding more information about Florida.

At the newspaper office, Max dropped in on his old friend Chip Carswell. Carswell was sitting at a window overlooking Washington Street, and jumped up when he saw Max.

"Hey, Max. You're just the man I wanted to see."

"That usually means trouble," said Max.

"Care to comment on a case? As our local Sherlock, your opinion would be of interest to our readers."

"What case?"

"Right here. Came in on the wire about a week ago and it's still open, apparently. Someone murdered a local real estate guy in Jacksonville, Florida. The police think it might be a disgruntled client."

Max shrugged. "Well, they know a lot more about it than I do. Besides, what's so special about this case?"

"It has a little twist that would be right up your alley. The man was stabbed in a small locked room while he was shooting at the killer. Can you beat that?"

"Hmmm," said Max, looking at the brief article. "Interesting, but a long way from here and I don't have any real information, so I don't have anything to say."

"I thought the readers would be interested in your impressions."

"Your readers enjoy reading uninformed opinion, do they?"

"I would hardly call your opinion uninformed. Why you're practically an expert in criminal matters."

"Thank you very much. You make me sound like a burglar."

"You know what I mean, Max," Carswell insisted. "The killer stabbed an armed man in a locked room and then disappeared. Why, it's sensational. It's irresistible. The man must be a magician. You have to have an opinion."

"You want an opinion?" said Max. "Here it is. I have never known a magician to be a murderer. Besides, magic is illusion, and I'm sure this murder is a simple illusion as well. It only seems to be magic because you do not immediately see how it was done."

"All right, all right. I understand," said Carswell, holding up his hands. "Maybe you can help me with another problem."

"Another case I don't know anything about?"

"Nah, just a little dilemma, sort of."

"I hate it already."

"You remember Bubba Henderson from school?"

Max nodded. "I was just telling Allison about him yesterday. Bubba was hard to forget. How many people singed their own eyebrows off in chemistry lab?"

"Yeah, and don't forget the time Bubba brought a cow to the schoolyard."

Max grimaced. "It took a week to get the place cleaned up afterwards. Yeah, old Bubba had a way of keeping the pot boiling, all right."

"Well," said Carswell, lowering his voice, "It seems Bubba has disappeared."

"What do you mean? I thought he was living in Annapolis."

"He's running a buy boat out of there. He buys up the catch from the watermen working the oyster beds in the bay and sells it in Annapolis or Baltimore."

"So he disappeared?"

"Nobody's seen him for over a week. Somebody called me yesterday to see if I'd heard anything. Max, I don't know what to think. I always liked Bubba. He lent a certain air to the place back in school."

"Especially the day he brought the cow to school," Max remarked. "Maybe he's still despondent about losing the hall monitor job."

"Anyway, I've been asking around and this one old boy told me he heard a waterman's been making threats against old Bubba-claims Bubba cheated him on some oysters."

Max looked at Carswell suspiciously.

"Chip, are you serious? Bubba wasn't the smartest guy on God's green earth, but I never figured him for a crook."

"Me neither, Max, but the fact remains, he's missing. Do you think you could look into it?"

"Come on, Chip. I don't do missing persons cases. For that you need the real police. They have access to all the records and can arrest people. If Bubba turns up murdered, give me a call."

"Look, Max; you have a way of getting to the bottom of things."

"So does sludge. I can't think of a bigger waste of time than chasing after Bubba Henderson."

"Max," said Carswell, "remember when I did you a big favor?"

"No, I don't."

"Well, we've known each other for years; I must have done something."

"You're doing it now. You're annoying me. "

"Alright, Max. I'll level with you. My editor is convinced there's foul play going on and he's breathing down my neck to dig out the story. If I don't come up with something soon, I could be in trouble here. Max, I'm begging you; help me out on this one and I'll be in your debt."

Max looked out the window at an ice truck lumbering up Washington Street and sighed. "All right, Chip. I'll ask around a bit, but it's not my area and I'm not promising anything."

"That's fine., Max," said Carswell. "As long as you're looking at it, there's some hope. The police aren't interested. They say Bubba's disappeared before. They think he's on a bender somewhere."

"Now, how could that be?" Max asked. "Alcohol's illegal."

"Of course. How could I forget?" Carswell snickered.

"Well, give me the name of the palooka that says Bubba cheated him and we'll start from there."

"Here it is. Nelson Udall. He lives near Royal Oak, across from Oxford."

"So now you're a missing person's bureau?" Allison asked on the way home.

"Pretty degrading, huh? Just a few years ago I solved a triple murder, now I'm looking for a renegade ex-hall monitor. I'll be searching for lost cats next."

"You're going to question the guy who said Bubba cheated him?"

"It's a start. I'll just have to see. So how was your expedition?"

"The Easton library has a few books on Florida, but they're so old I think they were written by Ponce De Leon himself. I can't find anything that's up to date."

"So what about your article?"

"Well, if I can't get someone to sponsor a trip, I may not be able to get enough up to date information to do an article. I may have to give it up. I do have one lead, a local man named Newton Wilson who lives on the St Michaels Road who lost his shirt down there. I may talk to him and see where it leads."

"I have a man to talk to about Bubba over in Royal Oak. Maybe we can go together."

John Reisinger

Chapter 5
Death on Lake George

On the shore of Lake George in Central Florida, meanwhile, Jake, the owner of Jake's Marina and Boat Rental Service had a missing person of his own to deal with. Pacing up and down the pier, he looked out over the darkening waters of the lake and noticed the sun was getting low. He frowned and looked at his pocket watch. Shadows were lengthening; it would be dark in less than an hour and the sky to the west already was showing streaks of orange and red. He was almost ready to close up for the day, but there was still one bit of unfinished business to deal with first.

"Mr. Godfrey is usually back long before this. I wonder if he's having trouble with his outboard again?"

He squinted towards the northeast, where Mr. Godfrey usually went to fish. Jake knew Mr. Godfrey had a favorite spot he went to all the time. Fishermen were like that, even if the results weren't always encouraging. He could see the silhouette of Mr. Godfrey still sitting quietly in his boat.

He picked up his old binoculars and scanned the lake. There were only a few boats out and the surface looked peaceful enough, but he knew Mr. Godfrey was overdue.

Jake looked in the direction of the cove and scanned the surface until he focused on a dark silhouette in the distance.

"There he is," Jake muttered. "Must be burned to a crisp bein' out there so long. He's not moving near as I can tell. Don't look like he's headin' in. Well, guess I'd better go see if he needs help."

Jake walked out on the rickety old dock, untied an old fishing boat and started up the outboard. He roared off in a cloud of bluish gray smoke from the old Evinrude. The v-shaped ripples of boat's wake sparkled in the calmness of the water. He didn't really mind chasing after Mr. Godfrey this way; Mr. Godfrey was a good customer. Besides, it was an excuse for a relaxing boat ride in the still of dusk.

In a few minutes, he could see Mr. Godfrey clearer. He was still sitting in a chair he had rigged up for fishing and was slumped down a little, as if he had gotten sleepy and nodded off.

Jake chuckled.

"Must have fallen asleep. That's why he didn't get back when he usually does. Well, the sun'll do that to you out on the lake. I'll just have to wake him up before he gets caught out here in the dark."

Godfrey's boat was anchored at the entrance to an inlet. It was a peaceful place, with a backdrop of heavily wooded shoreline and a lot of privacy. Jake could see why he liked the place. It was the closest thing to wilderness on the lake.

"Hey, Mr. Godfrey!" he called out, his voice echoing slightly in the stillness. "It's me; Jake from the marina. It's getting pretty late. You want to pack it in for the day? Thought you might like to..."

Jake stopped in mid-sentence.

Even in the fading light, he was close enough to see the blood.

Chapter 6
On the trail

The men Max and Allison wanted to interview proved somewhat elusive, since they were both watermen and the oyster season was still in full swing. Both men were out before dawn and did not return until well after dark on most days. Max didn't press the issue, since he knew better than to interfere in someone's livelihood, especially someone who lived as close to the line as a waterman.

So for several days, Max and Allison contented themselves with making a few casual phone inquiries and mining the ever-productive vein of Isis Dalrymple's inside information about nearly everyone. Finally, however, they arranged to meet both men one cold afternoon and set off down the St Michaels Road in the Model T.

Newton Wilson, the man who lost his savings in Florida land lived on a creek. He had agreed to talk to Allison when he found out she was writing a magazine article. He wanted to tell the world.

Wilson was a thin, nervous individual who chain smoked and mumbled to himself on occasion. He lived in a small, neat house that smelled of tobacco. They sat in his parlor under the watchful eye of a white cat. Since it was too cold to wait outside, Max came in and stayed in the background.

"My life savings," Wilson muttered. "All of it gone. All I have left is the deed to a piece of property no one will buy, even at half of what I paid. It seemed like a sure thing. I did my research. People were getting rich overnight. People were selling for big profits after only a few days. But then it was over. It was like a game of musical chairs and I was standing when the music stopped."

"How did you find out about the land, Mr. Wilson," Allison asked.

"Newspaper ad. Here I still got it."

He pulled out a well-worn newspaper and showed her an advertisement.

Florida land! You can own a piece of paradise. Prime land in the Sunshine State. Special price: 10 acres for $150 for a limited time. Hurry-send your check today!

I bought 100 acres for only $1500, everything I had. I waited a few weeks, then tried to sell it, but there were no buyers. I don't know what to do with the place."

"Did you ever think or retiring there?"

Wilson got up and threw another log into his pot-bellied stove in the corner, then came back and sat down heavily.

"Oh, I don't think I ever really wanted to retire there, but I wanted to have the ability to retire there if I wanted to. I'm over sixty five now, and I guess I'll have to keep arsterin' until I drop dead. I never should have listened to that real estate crook down in Florida."

"Did he promise you you'd make money on the deal?" Allison asked.

"Well, to be honest, I can't say he came right out with a guarantee or nothin', but he did fill me with stories about how much other people were making.

Turns out the only one to make any money on the deal was the real estate man and the bank."

He sat back in the chair and sighed, then looked over at Allison.

"Say, you and your husband wouldn't be interested in some land at a bargain price, would ya?"

Nelson Udall was short, grizzled, and irritable. He returned from his oystering around five and was available to talk after he had his dinner. His house squatted among several other waterman's houses that had clearly been built at the same time. His workboat was tied up to a sturdy pier just outside. A few pieces of ice clung to the rails.

Max had told him he was looking into Bubba Henderson's "situation" for the newspaper.

"His situation? I'll tell you his situation. He's a damned crook. He tight packs when he buys and loose packs when he sells."

Allison, sitting in the small kitchen, looked at Max questioningly, but said nothing.

"He waits until you got a really big catch, then tight packs the arsters and pays you based on that. I never minded that so much, since he paid a fair price in the end, but then by the time he gets to the cannery, he has most of the catch loose packed. The people at the cannery complained and Bubba blames me! Now every time I bring in my own catch, the cannery people examine every bushel...like I'm a cheat or something."

"Have you seen Bubba since then?" said Max.

"Just once. He come up alongside and offered to buy my catch and I told him to stay away from me or I'd throw him over the side next time. I haven't seen him since."

"So you don't know where he might have disappeared to?"

"No, I don't, but I'll tell you one thing; wherever he is, I hope he stays there!"

"Well, those were two unhappy people," Max remarked on the way home.

"You said it," said Allison. "Say, what was all that about loose pack and tight pack?"

Max smiled. "Just some local chicanery. Oysters are sold by the bushel, not by weight. Well, some watermen, and some buy boat men know how to pack the oysters loose so they'll wind up with a few more bushels to sell. The buyers obviously prefer the oysters tightly packed in the bushel baskets, so they'll get their money's worth."

"Ah, the eternal give and take of the marketplace," said Allison.

Max chuckled. "Yes, your average waterman could teach a money lender a thing or two about practical economics."

Allison pulled her coat tighter.

"It's getting colder. Do you want to stop at the post office before we go home?"

Max nodded. "Sure. We're not far away."

They chugged into town and pulled up in front of the post office. They got the mail after passing some "Cold enough for you?" pleasantries with the postmaster then set off for home.

Allison thumbed through a pile of letters as they drove down the oyster shell road.

"Anything interesting?" Max asked.

"No. Just the usual bills and...hello, what's this?"

"What?"

"Now here's a coincidence. We've been talking about Florida and here you have a letter from there. Miami Springs, Florida, to be precise. Do we know anyone there?"

"Not a soul. It's probably a real estate pitch from someone trying to unload the property next to Mr. Wilson's. I wonder where they got my name?"

Allison shook her head and she tucked the letter back into the pile. "Well, no rush to read that one. After what I heard today, I'm almost afraid to open the thing. Maybe a little hand will come out and grab all our money. You know, Max, it's really a shame I can't get anyone to back a trip to Florida for my article. There certainly seems to be a lot going on down there. Apparently they're sending out letters to strangers now. They must be getting desperate."

"Things do seem to be percolating in the Sunshine State," Max replied. "Say why don't you open that letter from Miami Springs? Maybe someone is offering a good rate on a Florida hotel or something. Besides, I'm curious what their pitch might be."

"All right, but hold on to your wallet." Allison fished out the letter and tore it open.

"It's a business letter all right; typed and everything. It looks very official."

"So who's it from?"

She looked at the signature at the bottom of the page. She gasped slightly.

"Oh, Max. It can't be. There must be some mistake."

"So who sent the letter?"

She held up the page.

"Glenn Curtiss."

John Reisinger

Chapter 7
Curtiss

Max stopped the Model T by the side of the road and grabbed the letter.

"Glenn Curtiss? *The* Glenn Curtiss? The living aviation legend? The man who produced the Curtiss Jenny we fly around in? The rival to the Wright brothers? Why would Glenn Curtiss be writing to me?"

"Maybe he wants his airplane back. Maybe we're giving it a bad name."

Max didn't answer. He was devouring the letter. Finally, he looked up with a bewildered look on his face. He seemed to have forgotten all about how cold it was. Allison hadn't. She sat huddled, pulling her coat tightly around her.

"I don't believe it," Max said finally.

"So what does he say? I'd like to at least know before I freeze to death."

Max looked at the letter again, then handed it to Allison.

Dear Mr. Hurlock:

Having read of some of your exploits, I would very much like to meet you, and, of course, your wife. I believe your talents might prove invaluable if applied to a certain matter of urgency that has arisen and would like to discuss it with you in person. At this point, I can only say that it concerns a situation that could endanger scores of people and thousands of livelihoods.

Accordingly, I am inviting you and your wife to visit me in Florida, so we can discuss this important situation. You will be under no obligation to assist in this matter, but I do ask that you hear me out.

I will pay your expenses and any fees that may be appropriate, but ask that you keep this matter strictly confidential for now. If you will send me a confirming telegram at the below address, I will wire $300 to cover your immediate travel expenses.

I look forward to meeting you both.

Sincerely,

Glenn Curtiss

Miami Springs, Florida

P.S. I understand you fly one of my surplus Jennys. Good for you, but this time of year, I'd advise coming to Florida by train.

Some address and contact information followed.

Allison handed the letter back to Max.

"Max, are you certain this is on the up and up?"

"It sure looks like it. Look at the stationary, and I just read the other day that he was building a house in Miami Springs, Florida. But what would he want with me? What kind of situation could he be talking about?"

"I think it's safe to assume he hasn't murdered anybody," said Allison.

"Well, Allison; you were hoping someone would underwrite a trip to Florida. It looks like you got your wish."

"That's wonderful, but what about Bubba?"

"Bubba?"

"You know; the bird you're supposed to be looking for? Do you think you'll find him in Florida?"

"Oh....Bubba. Well, I'll make a few more inquiries, but I don't think there's much more I could do anyway.

Missing persons isn't my line of work and I'm at a dead end. Knowing Bubba, he probably gave up the water to head west and become a cowboy or something. There is absolutely no evidence of foul play so far, but I'll take the steamer to Annapolis tomorrow and ask around, just to cover all the bases. After that, I've done what I promised."

Max sent a telegram the next morning and the money from Florida arrived at the post office an hour later. Meanwhile Max took the steamship Cambridge to Annapolis to talk to some of the people who worked with Bubba Henderson.

While he was in Annapolis, Max, contacted the Baltimore and Ohio Railroad agent and arranged for two tickets south to Richmond with connections to the Southern Railroad to Florida. Then he set out to find someone who knew something about what had become of Bubba.

No one seemed to have any idea what happened to Bubba and no one could recall Bubba giving any hint he was contemplating a change of scene.

Joe Bartlet, the owner of the pier where Bubba kept his buy boat scratched his unshaven chin thoughtfully.

"Bubba? Well, can't rightly say. Bubba didn't talk about future plans much. Bubba just sort of went about his business best he could."

"How was his business?"

Bartlet shrugged. "He got by mostly. Of course what with the fluctuations in the price of oysters, sometimes old Bubba got caught flat footed and had to eat the difference. He doesn't own that boat, you know. He rents it, and that makes it even harder to make any money. He used to say he needed to find some place where the prices were more stable and the weather wasn't as bad. Say, that's his boat over there. You can take a look if you want."

"Thanks. I think I will."

Max felt the boat shift slightly with his weight as he climbed on board. The boat had been cleaned recently and showed no signs of oysters except for a lingering smell. Max went into the small pilot house near the stern.

The pilot house was in good order. A wooden wheel was at the center and some compartments and shelves lined each side with an elevated bunk in the back. In a drawer on the port side, Max found a log book. Pressed between the pages were about a dozen receipts from packing houses for loads Bubba had sold. The newest one was dated about the time Bubba disappeared.

Max pulled out the receipt and examined it. On a hunch, he went through the other drawers until he found a pile of receipts for oysters Bubba had bought directly from watermen. He found the one from the same day and matched it up with the packing house paper.

Max shook his head. That day, Bubba had made exactly fifty cents on a bushel of oysters, and had a total of 90 bushels. That came out to 45 dollars for a hard day's work. By the time he paid for his diesel oil, Bubba would have been lucky to break even. No wonder he sometimes resorted to the loose pack trick; he was trying to survive. Max put the papers back where he had found them, feeling slightly guilty for prying into his old friend's troubles.

The more he thought about it, the more likely it seemed that there was no foul play involved; Bubba had simply gotten discouraged with the frustrations of working on the bay and cleared out for greener pastures. Well, good luck to him. There was nothing more to be done.

As Max closed the log book, a piece of paper fell out and fluttered to the floor. He picked it up and was surprised to see it was a newspaper clipping. An attractive woman in a bathing suit stretched out beneath a palm tree and words that seemed somehow familiar.

Come to Florida and live the good life!
The land of sunshine and clear blue waters is
waiting for you.
Stake out your claim to Paradise. Florida land is
the investment of a lifetime.

John Reisinger

Chapter 8
The Sunshine State

"Look Max. A palm tree! I haven't seen one of those since we were in Jekyll Island a few years ago. Florida is going to be the bee's knees."

Allison was looking out the window of the Southern Railway car and taking in the passing scenery. Beside her, Max sat reading a newspaper.

Max looked up. "I think we're still in Georgia, but it does look nice after the ice and snow in St Michaels."

She sat back contentedly. "This is wonderful. I get to find first hand background for my article and you get to meet one of your idols. This is unusual for you, Max. You don't go in for hero-worship as a rule."

"It's true I have very little use for movie stars, politicians, and celebrities in general," Max admitted, "but I do admire people who actually accomplish something substantial, and Curtiss is close to the head of that list."

"What do you suppose he wants you to do? Do you suppose it has something to do with flying?"

Max put the paper down. "I doubt it. What help could he possibly need from me about flying? That would be like Will Rogers asking me how to be funny."

"Maybe he wants you to do an advertisement with Gypsy; something like 'A Curtiss airplane gets me to the crime scene faster.' You could wear a leather jacket and a white scarf blowing in the breeze."

Max snickered. "Sure, and you can be my agent. Anyway, Curtiss sold his interest in Curtiss Company several years ago. That's why he moved to Florida. I understand he's still doing some aircraft inventing, but he's also developing land around Miami."

"Maybe he wants you to give him some engineering advice."

"Well, we'll just have to wait and see. Meanwhile, let's enjoy the scenery. We'll be in St Augustine in a few hours. We spend the night at the Alcazar Hotel, then go the rest of the way to Miami in the morning."

Allison squeezed his arm. "A hotel? Great. That will give us a chance to work on the Max, Jr. project."

The Alcazar Hotel in St Augustine was an elaborate Moorish-themed palace in the center of town. The lobby was a riot of arches, heavy oak furniture, carved woodwork, and Persian carpets.

"Nice place," said Max. "I wonder if Ali Baba stays here when he's in town?"

"Just stay away from the Harem," Allison replied.

The desk clerk was expecting them and had a telegram for Max.

"It's from Glenn Curtiss," said Max. "He says a driver will pick us up at the station in Miami and that we are to be his guests for dinner tomorrow night."

"Dinner with Glenn Curtiss?" said Allison. "First an expenses paid trip to Florida, then this. It sounds like you won the Lifebuoy Soap Contest."

Max shook his head. "Whatever Curtiss wants me to do must be something really distasteful to pull out all the stops this way."

"Or really important, more likely."

That night, they smelled the warm flower-scented tropical air from the comfort of a very large bed. The arches, heavy curtains and Arabesque wall hangings around them, barely visible in the darkness, continued the exotic theme of the lobby. Stars twinkled through the open windows.

Max sighed and pulled Allison a little closer. "Well, whatever Curtiss wants me to do, it's worth it being here with you."

Allison kissed him on the cheek. "I'll bet you say that to all the princesses."

When the train arrived at the station in Miami the next afternoon, a limousine was waiting beneath several palm trees. A chauffeur stood beside it holding a sign that said simply "HURLOCK". The driver gathered up Max and Allison's luggage and opened the door for them. Then they were off through the sun-dazzled streets of Miami.

Blue waters sparkled here and there as they passed blocks of Spanish style white stucco houses with red tile roofs set among beds of flowers and palm trees. Finally, they passed a sign that said Welcome to Miami Springs. The limousine soon came to a large rambling adobe structure that looked like it might have come from New Mexico. Some workmen were busily applying stucco to one wall while a crew was planting palm trees around the other side. The limousine passed through an arched entrance leading to an inner courtyard. The driver opened the door and escorted them inside to a plush sitting room that looked as if it had come from the Alcazar.

The chauffeur left the room and Max and Allison looked at each other.

"Now what?" said Allison. "Is this another hotel?"

Max shook his head. "It's small for a hotel but big for a house. I guess we'll just have to wait and..."

"Mr. and Mrs. Hurlock?" came a voice. "Welcome to Miami Springs. I'm Glenn Curtiss."

Max spun his head around to see a thin man with a thick mustache entering the room. The man wore a plain tweed suit and bristled with nervous energy. Max stood up.

"It's an honor to meet you, Mr. Curtiss. I'm Max Hurlock and this is my wife Allison."

"Thank you both for coming. This is my home in Miami Springs. You can see it isn't finished yet, but it's comfortable. I'd like you both to stay here for the next two nights if that's all right. I'd like you to keep a low profile in town for reasons I'll explain at dinner."

Max nodded. "Of course."

"Arnold will show you your room. Your luggage is already there. I know you must be tired from your trip, so why don't you both freshen up a bit and I'll see you at dinner in about an hour."

Allison sat in a Spanish style carved chair in their room and threw her hat on the canopied bed.

"One thing you have to say about this case, if it really is a case that is; you can't beat the accommodations."

Max looked out the window at a low skyline of partly completed buildings.

"But why the secrecy? Who did he expect to see us and what difference would it make? Well, Glenn Curtiss isn't one to be sloppy or leave things to chance, so I suppose he has his reasons."

"No doubt" Allison agreed. "I just wish we knew what they were.

"So how do you like your Jenny, Max?" Curtiss asked. Max, Allison, Curtiss, his wife Lena, and two other men Curtiss had introduced as James Bright and

D.P. Davis were seated around a lavishly appointed dinner table and a meal of roast beef. Davis was shorter and stockier than Curtiss, and was clean shaven. A sea breeze drifted through the room from the open windows, carrying a faint salt smell.

"It's fine airplane, sir."

"Call me Glenn, for heaven sakes."

"All right. Anyway we've had a lot of great flying and a few adventures with our Jenny."

"Well, we certainly made enough of them. We've come a long way since Orville and Wilbur flew at Kitty Hawk. That was the first manned heavier than air flight, although I proved that Professor Langley's aerodrome would have flown much earlier with a few modifications. Then I had the first *public* heavier than air powered flight a little later, but Wilbur and Orville were the first officially."

"And they've been filing lawsuits against you ever since," Lena added.

"Yes, well they're trying to protect their patents after all, and being first is critical for that. Personally, I'd rather expend my energies developing new airplane innovations than fighting about old ones, but the Wright boys don't see it that way, so the lawsuits have been a big drain on my time and money. Even so, we've turned out some pretty good aircraft since then, including the America flying boat, the first airplane to fly the Atlantic. No one has done it solo yet, but that will come soon enough. The potential of aviation has barely been scratched."

Allison looked at Max. When was Curtiss going to get to the business at hand?

Max didn't care. He was talking to Glenn Curtiss, one of the world's greatest aviation pioneers; the first man to fly between cities, the first man to carry air mail, the inventor of ailerons, retractable landing gear, seaplanes, naval aviation, and a hundred other innovations. And Curtiss was treating him as an equal in a far ranging conversation that covered the sky. Max was in heaven. Occasionally, Lena would guide the conversation towards current events to engage with Allison, but the talk always drifted back to flying. Max didn't want it to end, but eventually, it did.

"Well, said Curtiss," as the cook cleared away the dishes, "I think I owe the Hurlocks an explanation for why I dragged them down here. Lena, why don't you show Allison the rest of the house while the men retire into the sitting room?"

"Uh, Glenn," said Max. "Unless it's something indelicate, I'd like Allison to come along. I find her perspective can often be invaluable."

Curtiss smiled. "Well then why don't we all go into the sitting room? This concerns Lena as well.

A minute later they were comfortably seated in the room Max and Allison had first seen earlier. Curtiss wasted no time.

"Max, I didn't ask you to come down here to discuss flying. I need your help in a matter that's more your area of expertise. As you may know, I sold my interest in the Curtiss Company several years ago and came to Florida. Since then I've been helping to develop the area around Miami. In addition to Miami Springs, there's Opa-Locha and several others, including the Hialeah Race track not far from here. Jim Bright here is my partner in the Curtiss-Bright Development Company."

Max nodded. He was aware of most of this already.

"Now D.P. Davis here does the same thing a little further north around Tampa and St Augustine. He's currently developing Davis Shores, a planned community of Spanish style houses with a hotel, restaurant, boat docks, and all the amenities."

"And there was nothing there but swamp before I started," D.P. chimed in. "Now it's a budding community."

"It's a beautiful place," Bright chimed in. "Glenn and I have gotten some good ideas from D.P. I like to think we're making Florida a better place."

"Absolutely," Curtiss added. "The point is, we are building the future of Florida because we believe in this area. But I'm sure you know about the reverses we've had lately. People bought land just as speculation, counting on selling it for a fat profit in just a few days. Well, that bubble is bursting and there are a lot of unhappy people who blame us for their bad decisions. We can survive the bad press, but now there is a new factor."

Curtiss paused. "It seems someone is murdering Florida developers and real estate people and is doing it in a spectacular way that is sure to bring attention. I'd like to get your opinion on the case, Max."

"I assume you're talking about the murder of Mr. Russo some weeks ago," said Max.

"Yes; a head scratching locked room murder if ever there was one. What's your opinion of the case?"

"I don't have an opinion. There's not enough information available. I find if you form an opinion before you have all the facts you'll start slanting the facts to fit the opinion instead of the other way round."

"Hmmm. Then I suppose you have no opinion on the Bill Godfrey murder either."

"I didn't know about that one," said Max.

"He was a small developer, but was pretty successful around the Orlando area. He went out fishing on Lake George in full view of a marina and was bludgeoned to death. Nobody saw or heard a thing. So now we have two Florida real estate men in just a few weeks, killed in mysterious ways guaranteed to draw attention."

"And you think these two crimes are related?" Max asked.

"No one knows for sure, but the papers are starting to play up the Florida real estate angle and how clever the killer is. A few are referring to the killer as 'The Invisible Man' because no one ever sees him. My concern is that if whoever is doing this is getting back for his losses, he'll keep killing, and he might get a lot of sympathy and even look like a hero to some people. We can't let a killer rally the public to think all Florida real estate is a bad investment just because a few people went too far out on a limb and lost money. We especially can't let the public start to associate Florida land with murder. We depend on settlers and on vacationing families to keep things moving along."

D.P. Davis took up the narrative. "The market will take care of flushing out the fly-by-night land salesmen down here. We don't need a killer to do the job."

"And that's why I asked you to come down here, Max," Curtiss said. "I want you to investigate and find out who's behind this and stop him. Otherwise it'll be chaos down here. We've worked too hard and too long to see Florida get dragged through the mud."

In spite of himself, Max was stunned. "Look, I'm just a small town guy from Maryland. You could afford anybody. You could hire the Burns Agency. Why me?"

"Simple. I know your background. You're a good investigator and you're discrete. You're not a glory hunter; you just get the job done. The fact that you're also a flier is just icing on the cake. Anyway, Burns was head of the Bureau of Investigation until a few months ago and now he's mixed up in that Teapot Dome scandal. He'd draw attention wherever he shows his face. We don't need that. Besides, he's not a flyer."

"What about the police?" said Max.

"The police are having a hard time figuring out how the killer committed the crimes, let alone who he is. Even if they do catch a good suspect, they'll have the devil's own time proving he did it if they can't even explain *how* he did it."

"I meant how will I get the cooperation of the police? They usually don't care for an outsider nosing in their business."

"That's covered. I talked to Governor Martin and he promised to have his people contact the appropriate police departments to let them know that you are being sent as a consultant to help them. They'll still be in charge, but they've been assured of your discretion. They'll get all the credit when the case is done. You'll be given a list of all the appropriate police agencies and whom to contact. You'll be paid expenses plus whatever fees you think are appropriate. You will also be provided with an automobile to get around in. Where you go and when will be up to you."

"Wait a minute," said Max. "If this killer is going after developers all over the state, there could be a dozen police departments or sheriff's offices involved. It'll be chaos. Isn't there anyone coordinating the investigation?"

"The governor has informally asked St John's County Sheriff Roy G. Atley in St Augustine to head up the effort and coordinate, since the first murder took place in his area and the other murder was not far away, but we're still trying to downplay the whole thing. If it keeps up, however, it will be a public relations nightmare."

Max nodded. "I can imagine."

"All right, then. Is there anything else you think you might need to get started?"

"I'll need a list of real estate developers, real estate agents, investors, what lots are for sale, plus any files of hostile correspondence you've received; not just here, but statewide."

Curtiss turned to D.P. Davis. "See D.P.? I told you Max knew his stuff. The police still haven't asked for that information statewide. Well, we have that information, but there's so much of it that you'd need an army division to go through it. Still, it's a start."

Max looked at Allison, who appeared almost as surprised as he was.

"I think I'll need a good sized map of Florida, one that has the major developments shown and the names of the developers. Of course the murder sites should be marked as well. Oh, and some local newspaper clippings about the murders would be helpful."

Curtiss turned to Davis. "What do you think, D.P.? Can we get that together for Max?"

D.P. nodded. "I'll have it ready tomorrow morning, along with the other material Max needs."

Lena spoke for the first time.

"Allison, I'm sure you can understand this. All those years Glenn was risking his life flying in experimental airplanes and in constant danger of disaster, I worried about him. I never knew if he was going to come home or not. Now that that's finally behind him, I refuse to possibly lose him to some deranged killer. Nor do I intend to stand by while all the good work he's done in Florida is undermined by some psychopath with a flair for publicity. Max, you do whatever you have to do and tell us whatever you need, but stop him!"

Chapter 9
Tin can tourists

When Max and Allison got back to their room, they sat in silence for a few minutes, trying to grasp what had just happened. Finally, Allison spoke.

"Well, Max, your friend Glenn Curtiss seems to have a lot of faith in you. This is a tough assignment."

"Tough? Not at all," Max replied. "I just have to track an invisible man across the entire state of Florida. Nothing to it."

"Do you think you can do it? Is there a chance?"

"Oh, there's a chance, all right. In fact, there are two chances; slim and unlikely."

"So where do you start?"

Max seemed lost in thought. "What? Oh. Well, I'll need to visit the murder sites and see if I get any ideas. I'll also look through the lists of disgruntled investors and see if anything pops up. Of course everyone is assuming that a disgruntled investor is to blame, but it might be someone else altogether."

Allison put her arm around him.

"Poor Max. Looking for a needle in a haystack is bad enough, but you're looking for a needle in a dozen haystacks."

"Well, then I'd better get started first thing tomorrow. We'll take the automobile Glenn promised and hit the road for Jacksonville to visit the scene of

Mr. Russo's demise, then Lake George to find out what happened on Mr. Godfrey's fishing expedition."

"And I should be able to pick up all sorts of Florida lore along the way," said Allison. "The article should be a cinch."

"So," said Max, as they prepared for bed, "wouldn't it be great if Max, Jr got his start in Glenn Curtiss's house?"

Allison switched off the light.

"Prepare for takeoff," she whispered.

The automobile promised by Glenn Curtiss turned out to be a new Packard. Max and Allison carefully packed it and set off for Jacksonville the next morning. Since he took the train down to Miami Springs, D.P. Davis accepted Max's invitation to ride back with them. St Augustine was close to Jacksonville and Max figured he could save time by getting a lot of background information from Davis.

The two lane winding road roughly followed the railroad along the coast up to Daytona, where the railroad headed off northeast to Palatka. One of the first things Max and Allison noticed were the abundance of overloaded vehicles headed in both directions.

"Tin can tourists," Davis explained. "People from up north come down here on vacation, but don't have the money for the big hotels like the Royal Poinciana in Palm Beach or the Breakers in Miami, so they sort of camp out in campgrounds or tourist courts. They call them tin can tourists because they carry tin cans of provisions, like they're headed out west. Some even come here homesteading, intending to build on a building lot they bought by mail."

"Do they really know what they're getting into?" Allison asked.

Davis sighed. "Many of them don't. They're in love with the idea of Florida, but haven't got much of a feel for the reality. Some of them run out of money and head back north. Even worse, some of them head back north and run out of money along the way. They wind up in Georgia in South Carolina in sort of refugee camps."

They were passing Port Lucie Inlet, north of Palm Beach when Max spotted a sign offering building lots for sale on easy credit.

"I suppose that kind of advertising is part of the problem."

Davis agreed. "Yeah. There's a lot of fly-by-nights, I'm afraid. Now at Davis Shores, we have some pretty slick advertising too, mind you. The difference is that we don't promise more than we can deliver."

"But you still have defaults at Davis Shores?" Max asked.

"We're starting to."

"Do some of them turn on the developer?"

"A few," Davis answered. "They think they've been swindled, or that the rich developer should reimburse them, or at least share in the losses. Funny thing is, nobody insisted on sharing their profits with the developer when they were making money on resales."

They stopped for the night at a boarding house Davis knew north of Melbourne. The landlady, a wiry lifelong Florida resident, provided an excellent chicken dinner and they were feeling so refreshed after the long drive that Max and Allison went for a walk along the beach before turning in. The moon had risen and the sand dunes seemed to glow in the soft gray light.

"A romantic place," Allison remarked, grasping Max's arm.

"Just what we need," said Max. "I hope the bed doesn't squeak."

"We'll soon find out."

"Of course, the place would be more romantic if there weren't some nut running around killing people."

"Oh, I'm sure you'll soon fix that," said Allison.

"I don't know. That drive today reminded me just how big Florida is. There's a lot of ground to cover and a lot of places to hide."

"Well, I'm sure you...What's that?"

Max looked where she was pointing and saw a glow over the next sand dune.

"Let's have a look."

Beyond the next dune was a large wooded area lit by several dozen small fires and containing a wide assortment of automobiles, trucks, tents, and people. A sign on an access road was readable in the moonlight:

TAYLOR'S TOURIST CAMP
WELCOME TIN CAN TOURISTS

"We've struck the mother lode of tourists, it seems. Let's see what's going on."

The soft flickering light of campfires lit faces of people sitting in folding chairs in front of automobiles and tents. Most were casually dressed. Soft voices came from several directions at once, and children occasionally ran across the path.

"You folks new here?" came a voice.

Max and Allison turned to see a heavy set middle aged man emerge from just ahead on the dirt path. He was carrying some fresh-caught fish in a basket.

"Sort of. We're staying at the boarding house and thought we'd have a look at a real tourist camp," said Max.

"Well, you've come to the right place. Taylor's is the berries."

"Are all these people vacationing, or are they real estate investors?"

"Oh, I'd say mostly vacationers. Some of 'em on their first big automobile trip, but some are here looking for something a little more permanent."

"Like land to build on?"

"Or land to make a profit on."

"Do you know anyone like that?" Max asked.

"Sure. Old Tom Haven over there. Hey, Tom."

An older man emerged from the shadows.

"Finally caught some fish, I see."

"Never mind the fish. These folks are asking if anyone here is buying and selling Florida real estate."

Tom Haven smiled. "You in the market to buy a nice building lot around here?"

Allison piped up. "Not really. I'm Allison Hurlock and I write magazine articles. Right now I'm researching one on the Florida real estate boom and how people are making or losing money out of it."

"Oh, well. Come on over to my tent and sit down a spell."

Max knew that when it came to getting people, especially men, to tell all, there was a time to back off and let Allison take over. So they followed Tom Haven a short distance to a tent by a small campfire , a folding table still showing the remnants of dinner, and a ring of folding camp chairs. Max and Allison sat down, feeling like pioneers of the old west.

"The wife is over at the Jacksons' playing bridge," said Haven, settling into a somewhat larger chair, "so we can have a nice chat. Now, let's see; it was almost two years ago when I met my first Binder Boy..."

"Your first what?" said Allison, clearly confused.

The man chuckled. "Oh. I guess you don't know. When things were really hopping and they couldn't sell property fast enough, the real estate people didn't have time to meet every buyer personally, so most of the time they sent some college student helper to the lot with the papers to meet the buyer. They called them Binder Boys because they took a binder, or down payment for the land. They got a commission when the check cleared. Yeah, they really had an assembly line going when it came to property sales."

"So how did you find out about the land in the first place?" Max asked. He figured Allison had gotten Tom Haven sufficiently softened up by this time.

"Like most people, I guess. They put ads in northern newspapers and word of mouth does the rest. It looked foolproof, and for a while it was, but things are really tightening up lately."

"I suppose some people are not happy about that."

Haven picked up a stick and stirred the fire, sending sparks twisting upward into the night air.

"Well, I kept my buying under control; only spending what I could afford you understand. Some folks though got greedy and plunked their life savings down hoping for a killing on a quick resale. Some of them are getting foreclosure notices instead."

Haven paused, as if not sure if he should continue. Then he did.

"I even heard tell that some people have threatened some of the real estate folks. They say money is the root of all evil, but it's been my experience that the real root of all evil is the *lack* of money."

Chapter 10
A big crime in a small room

Max and Allison dropped D.P. Davis off at his office in St Augustine and checked back into the   Alcazar. For the first time in several days, they were alone.

"So what are your plans, Max? We have to get started. You have a killer to track down and I have an article to rustle up."

Max sat next to her on the bed and put his arm around her.

"What are your plans after that, I mean."

"We have to do our best for Max, Jr."

"Remind me tonight," she said. "But we have the entire afternoon first."

Max looked at his pocket watch. "I might have time to see the local sheriff coordinating the investigation. Davis says his name is Roy G. Atley and he's arranged a meeting in Atley's office at two."

"I'm sure you'll be as welcome as a hurricane to Mr. Atley," Allison remarked. "Nothing like a Yankee know-it-all dropping in to warm the heart of the Dixie contstabulary."

"We will see," said Max. "Meanwhile I suppose you will be starting on another literary quest for truth and enlightenment?"

"That's right. I'll be getting information together for an article on the truth behind the Florida land boom. I thought I'd start by strolling around town and maybe looking up some local newspaper or real estate people."

Max looked out the window at the palm trees and the skyline of St Augustine.

"Then we can meet back here for some dinner and some...er relaxation... the Max, Jr project, you know..."

"Oh, I know, but work before pleasure, and I have a feeling you're heading for more work than you realize."

The St John's County Sherriff's office, Max thought, looked pretty much like every other sheriff/police office he'd ever been to. There were some shabby looking desks and filing cabinets scattered under several glaring overhead lights. On each desk was a typewriter, a coffee cup, and piles of papers and folders. Large electric fans were scattered about, stirring up the humid air and causing everyone to use various paperweights on their filing systems. Most desks had rocks or pieces of brick to hold papers in place, but some used books, ashtrays, and one pile of papers was held down by on old artillery shell.

Sheriff Roy G. Atley had a small office separated by a glass wall. The sheriff was a surprisingly young man who looked barely old enough to shave. He was tall and thin and wore his black hair parted in the middle. He wore a black suit with a badge on the vest.

"How are you doin', Mr. Davis?"

"Morning, Sheriff. Max, this is Sheriff Roy Gabriel Atley, known around here as Sheriff Roy G. Sheriff, this is Max Hurlock. The governor and Glenn Curtiss have asked him to help out in the Russo and Godfrey cases."

Atley looked warily at Max and nodded. "I know," he said flatly. "I got a call from the governor's office yesterday. They said Mr. Hurlock here is to pretty much have the run of the place. Kinda unusual. Not the way I usually work. Having someone new dropped into an investigation like this one is asking for trouble, especially somebody from up north, who doesn't know a palmetto from a pine nut about Florida, but I suppose the governor knows what he's doing. No offense, Mr. Hurlock."

"None taken, Sheriff."

"Mr. Hurlock here," Davis began, "has been involved in a number of murder cases as a consultant to the police. He has an admirable record of finding killers. He solved a double murder in a locked room up in New Jersey a couple of years ago and found out who killed that Connelly fellow up in New York City."

Atley nodded, but showed no expression. "That so?"

"And this is important. He is discrete. No announcements and no crowing to the press. Mr. Hurlock works quietly. Whatever he finds out, you'll hear it first, and you'll get the credit."

Atley was suddenly interested.

"Is that a fact? Well, I suppose that sounds good, but if he's so danged discrete, how come Mr. Curtiss and Governor Martin know all about him?"

Davis was at a loss for words, but Max laughed.

"Very good, sheriff. You have a flair for quick deductive reasoning. It's a fair point. The fact is, I do not seek publicity, but the word sometimes gets out none the less. I can't promise I'll be as invisible as our killer, but I will do what I can to stay out of the limelight. I am not here to take over. It's still your case, but Mr. Curtiss asked me to help because he figures it never hurts to have another pair of eyes."

Atley nodded. "Well, Hurlock, you're honest, at least, so I'll return the favor. I've hit a dead end with this case, so I can use any help I can get. I not only don't know who did it, I can't even tell you *how* he did it."

Max nodded sympathetically. "It does seem confusing from what I've read. Would it be possible to visit the crime scene?"

"I've been there twice already, but I suppose you need to see it as well. Don't see as it'll do any harm. It's just a few miles away. I was fixin' to take a run out there today myself. You can tag along if you'd like."

"And do you have photographs of the crime scene?"

"A folder full. I'll bring 'em along."

As they walked to the sheriff's car, Max and Atley passed a newsboy hawking the Jacksonville paper. Atley picked one up.

"Would you look at this?" Atley frowned, holding the paper up for Max to see, "The papers are going nuts over this case. I gotta work in a damned fishbowl. Just take a look at this headline.

WHO IS THE INVISIBLE MAN?
Police baffled by elusive killer
Where will he strike next?

Max looked back at Atley.

"Well, I suppose we'll just have to find out, won't we?"

"I have to find out, Hurlock," Atley retorted, "but maybe you can help out some."

Russo's Real Estate office stood in a Jacksonville outlying area sprinkled with palm trees. In spite of the death of the former owner, the office seemed busy. People looked up from their parallel rows of desks, but said nothing. They had gotten used to police visits by this time.

"Near as we can figure, the killer came in by the side door and then came down this aisle between the rows of desks. Russo's office was down at the end there. We didn't see any sign of a break in, but Russo never locked the outside door, so anybody could have walked right in."

They approached the office.

"Now, it's plain that Russo was stabbed, and just as plain that he had a gun handy and fired at the killer. Then it gets a little fuzzy."

He opened the door to a tiny office, little more than a closet. A desk stood in the center and Max could see that no point in the room was more than eight to ten feet from anyone sitting there.

"As you can see," Atley continued, gesturing, "if you shot at someone in the room while sitting at the desk, it would be pretty hard to miss. Hell, you'd probably get powder burns on the walls at this range. But there was no bullet, and no blood anywhere in the room except the blood soaked into Russo's sweater and a couple of streaky hand prints on the desk."

"Were they Russo's hand prints?"

"Looks like it. He had blood on both his hands. Here, take a look at the photos."

Max examined the photos and compared them to the now-cleaned–up room. He walked next to the desk and placed his hand where the handprint had been found, then he sat in the desk chair and looked at various angles. Finally, Max went to the door and examined the key.

"I don't see any photos of this key in the office door, sheriff. Didn't they take one?"

Atley scratched his head. "Come to think of it, I don't think they did. Why?"

"I was just wondering if there was any blood on the key?"

"As you can see, the key is one of those clunky old fashioned kinds, and was sort of a dark brown color anyway, so it would have been hard to tell."

Max nodded absently.

Atley continued. "And of course, there's the little matter of how the door got locked on the inside in the first place. As I said, the key was still in the keyhole inside, but the killer was gone. So a man gets shot and doesn't bleed, then escapes from a locked room without a trace."

"Why do you assume the killer was shot?" Max asked.

"Common sense, Hurlock. The gun had been fired, and there was no bullet found. That means the bullet had to be in the killer, and I don't think he caught it in midair somehow. You got any other explanation?"

Max didn't answer, but stood in the doorway frowning.

"I said, can you explain the lack of a bullet any other way?" Atley repeated.

"That's not what I'm wondering about," said Max. "I'm wondering why a man who doesn't bother to lock the front door of the building would lock the door to his office."

Atley looked momentarily surprised. "Well. It's too late to ask him. Maybe the killer locked it...just to bedevil us."

Max nodded. "Did your men check the rest of the office for blood or for the bullet?"

"We didn't even check Russo's office until days later when the coroner's report came out. Up until then it seemed like a clear case of suicide. When the coroner said Russo had been stabbed, we checked out the office pretty good; it had been locked up since the crime. There was no blood 'cept for Russo's, and no bullet anywhere."

"Good afternoon, gentlemen. Can I help?"

A short man with a thin mustache stood in the aisle outside the door. The office wasn't big enough for all of them.

"You remember me, don't you sheriff? I'm Hal Chester, the office manager."

"Oh, yes. Of course," said Atley. "How are you, Mr. Chester? This here's Max Hurlock. He's helping us out some."

"Have you found out anything else, sheriff?"

"We're working on it. That's why we're here; for another look."

"Mr. Chester," said Max, "could you check with whoever cleaned up the office and ask him if there was any sign of blood on the key?"

"The key?"

"That's right."

"I'll have to check. We had an outside cleaning service. I'll let the sheriff's office know what they say."

"Last time I talked with Mr. Chester," said Atley, "I asked him to check Mr. Russo's appointment book to see if he was supposed to meet anyone here the day he was murdered."

"A good question," said Max.

"But not such a good answer. Mr. Russo had no appointments on his calendar and no new names in his personal address book. No one in the office could recall seeing anyone new or suspicious hanging around, either."

"That would have been too easy. Has the floor been mopped since the crime, Mr. Chester?" Max asked.

"It's usually mopped every few days, but I told them to hold off in case the sheriff needed to investigate further. I read detective stories and I know that they can sometimes find clues from things dropped on the floor, like hairs or scraps of paper."

Max nodded with approval. "Very good thinking. And have you noticed anything like that?"

Chester's face fell. "Well, no. The place is kept pretty clean. I mean, there were no footprints or smudges or anything..."

"Too bad," said Max. "Well, thank you anyway. Sheriff, I think I'll just have a look around. You never know."

Max wandered out along the corridor looking at the floor. Mr. Chester looked at him, then at the sheriff.

"What's he doing, sheriff?"

"He's helping out. It's, uh, police business. Never mind. Now, was anyone in the company mad at Mr. Russo that you know of?"

"Well, Mr. Russo could be a little gruff and dismissive at times, but everyone here is used to that. If you're suggesting..."

Max was gesturing to them from the other end of the aisle. They reluctantly went to him.

Looks like your hunch was right, sheriff," said Max.

"My hunch?"

"You know; when you said I should search out here."

"Uhhh..." Atley was still not up to speed.

"Take a look at that," said Max.

"Did you know this was here, Mr. Chester?" Max was pointing to a small brown stain on one of the floorboards.

"No, but I guess somebody must have spilled a little coffee," Chester said.

60

"Oh, sure," grumbled Atley. "Maybe the killer had a cup of Joe after the stabbing to calm his nerves. Coffee stains. What next?"

The stain consisted of a small reddish brown spot of some dried liquid on the wooden floor near the front door, about 30 feet from Russo's office. Max kneeled down and looked at it closely.

"I tell everyone to be careful around here," said Chester, "but they walk around with cups of coffee sloshing over constantly. We get stains like that all the time. Of course, the floor's wood, so the stains don't really stand out that much. I just don't want anybody slipping on one."

Max nodded vaguely. "Uh huh. Say, sheriff, take a look at this would you?"

Atley squatted down reluctantly. "For God's sake, Hurlock. You want me to arrest someone for spilling his coffee?"

Max spoke softly so no one else would hear. "Take a closer look. Scrape a little bit up with your fingernail. Does that look or smell like coffee to you?" Max asked.

Atley sniffed and his eyes widened. "No. No, by God it doesn't. And look how dark and granular it is. It looks like..."

"Blood? That's the way it looks to me," said Max. "I'd say your hunch really paid off."

"If that's blood," said Atley, "then Russo must have at least winged the killer and he bled on his way out."

"Well, that's one possibility," said Max.

"What do you mean one possibility?" Atley demanded. "What else could it be?"

"Can your boys test this stain and identify the blood type?"

61

"What are we; Scotland Yard? We might be able to verify that the spot is blood if we're lucky, but that's all."

But Max wasn't listening. He had risen to his feet and was examining the wall area around the front door. Then Max started looking at some heavy curtains by an adjacent window.

"Now what?" Atley demanded. "Don't tell me you expect to find blood all the way over there?"

"This curtain has a hole in it." Max pulled the curtain aside. "And so does the wall behind it. Do you have a pen knife handy, sheriff?"

Atley produced a Boy Scout pen knife and started digging in the plaster. Suddenly, he stuck in his finger and pulled out a bullet.

"Well, what do you know? So that's where the bullet wound up," said Atley, poking at the slug in his palm. "But wait a minute. If this is the bullet that hit the killer, how did it wind up out here?"

"And," said Max, "how did the bullet get through the office door?"

"Maybe the door was open?" said Atley. "No. Wait a minute. If the door was open when Russo fired at the killer, who locked it afterwards? The killer was wounded and Russo was stabbed. It just doesn't make sense. I can't see any way that door could have been open when Russo fired. Even if the killer had some way of locking the door behind him, I can't see as how he'd take the time if he was bleeding from a bullet wound. And if he did somehow, why was his blood thirty feet away and not in Russo's office? What do you think, Max?"

Max picked up the bullet and looked at it a moment.

"I think we need to take a trip to Lake George."

Chapter 11
Davis Shores

Allison strolled along the river in St Augustine towards the old Spanish fort, now Fort Marion.

Fort Marion was an ominous grey stone structure on one end of town, bordering Matanzas Bay. It was a short walk from the hotel and since it also bordered the old colonial part of town, could be relied on to attract tourists. Although declared a National Monument two years ago, Fort Marion was still under the War Department and was still sitting vacant. That didn't stop the tourists from gawking and taking pictures, however, so Allison passed through the city gates at the end of George Street and started looking for subjects to interview.

Across Matanzas Bay she could see the tip of Anastasia Island with Davis Shores rising out of an old swampy area. A beautiful new bridge connecting the city with Davis Shores was under construction, but several small boat captains had posted signs offering a trip across the river for those who wanted a more elegant crossing, or who didn't quite trust the somewhat rickety-looking old wooden toll bridge that had been built in the previous century. Remembering the stories D.P. Davis had told of the place, Allison decided to interview tourists some other time and visit Davis Shores instead. D.P. Davis had recommended stopping at his St Augustine office to arrange a trip, so Allison found the address and asked about a tour.

"A tour?" said the man behind the desk. "Why, sure thing, little lady. Is your husband with you?"

Allison looked around. "No. It doesn't appear so."

"Well, maybe you could come back when he can come with you. You don't want to go alone."

"Oh? And why not? Are you expecting an alligator attack?"

"Well, suppose you find a great lot you'd like to buy. Why, you'd have to get him over there to sign the papers and write the check. And what if he doesn't approve? You'd just be wasting your time. You get your husband and we'll take you both on a royal tour. What do you say?"

Allison was tapping her foot in irritation by this time, but she smiled.

"I understand. Now that woman have the vote we can decide who will be president of the United States, but we still can't decide on a house by ourselves."

The clerk looked embarrassed. "Well,...I mean to say..."

"May I use your telephone? I'm sure my husband wouldn't mind."

"Oh, yes. Of course as long as it's a local call."

"Oh, it's very local."

While the clerk bustled about on the other side of the room Allison placed a call and spoke in a low voice. She replaced the receiver and stood quietly near the door. In a few seconds the phone rang and the clerk answered.

"Davis Shores Property Sales....yes....yes. Oh, good morning Mr. Davis. Yes...why yes, she is here. Well, I...that is I..Yes...Of course, Mr. Davis. Right away."

The clerk replaced the receiver and looked over at Allison.

"We have a boat leaving in ten minutes and there's a Davis Shores bus waiting on the other side. I'll escort you to the dock."

Allison smiled sweetly. "Thank you so much. That's very gracious of you."

An almost empty boat deposited Allison on a pier on the other side of the river a yellow bus with the words Davis Shores painted in red letters stood waiting. The bus driver greeted Allison and they were off.

"Isn't anyone else coming on this tour?" Allison asked.

"Well, things have been a little slow lately. Besides I got a call from Mr. Davis and he wants you to have the works."

Davis Shores had the look of a place that was being built from scratch, as it pretty much was. A handful of Spanish style houses and freshly planted flowerbeds shared winding streets with dusty vacant lots. Dump trucks carrying fill dirt rolled up and down the streets. A thin layer of brownish dust covered every horizontal surface. A grid of roads was laid out, but only partially paved. The bus bumped along mostly dirt thoroughfares.

"How are the sales going?" Allison asked.

The driver shrugged. "The sales are going fine, but they've slowed down temporarily. Of course, not everyone who buys here builds right away, so it's not as complete as the sales figures would indicate."

"Any forclosures?"

"Oh, I wouldn't know about that. I don't handle the financial end."

Allison noted that they had just passed a yard sign announcing a foreclosure auction.

"Yes Ma'am; just a few months ago, this place was just a mangrove swamp until Mr. Davis came along and filled it in. Now it's on its way to becoming the biggest neighborhood in St Augustine. Of course, it's still under construction and there's not many houses, but just give it time."

"Very impressive," said Allison. "Say, could you drop me off at the sales office?"

The driver grinned. "Sure thing. That's where I take everybody!"

The people in the sales office seemed to have been waiting for her. They jumped to their feet and offered her coffee, but added little to what the bus driver had said. Sales figures, apparently, were a delicate subject.

Allison left the office and strolled around the mostly empty streets of the development. There was a steady grinding hum in the air from dredges and steam shovels busy filling and extending the boundaries of the development into Matanzas Bay on the northeast side. The whole place was very much a construction project.

"Yoo hoo!"

Allison turned around and saw a woman about her age walking a dog. With the dog pulling at the leash, the woman caught up quickly.

"Are you new here?" the woman asked breathlessly.

"No; I'm just a visitor," Allison replied. "How about you?"

"Oh, I'm a pioneer, I guess. Name's Nancy. Me and Bill; that's my husband; we've been here for a couple of months. I was sort of hoping we were getting another neighbor."

"I'm afraid not. I'm more of a tourist. My name's Allison. So how do you like Davis Shores?" Allison asked as the dog sniffed her ankle.

Nancy shrugged. "It's fine so far, and it'll be even better when it gets some more people. But right now it's like a desert."

"It does look a little, well, uncrowded," said Allison. "Have you met Mr. Davis?"

"He dropped by one day after we moved in. Seemed like a nice enough fellow. No, he's not the problem. He just needs more customers and steadier payments from the ones he already has."

"Are you from Florida?"

Nancy chuckled. "Hardly anybody around here is. Bill and me, we came down from the north just like most people. We're just looking for a better life, I guess. Bill had this business, but it wasn't going well, and we thought we'd just drop everything and make a new start. So here we are. Bill's running a charter boat out of St Augustine. We're doing all right, but it sure gets lonely around here. How about you?"

"I'm here with my husband. He's on a project at the moment and I'm researching a magazine article about the Florida land boom."

"Well, honey, I could give you enough material for two articles. Say, I live just down the street. You see that house with the tree out front? What say you and your husband drop by for dinner Friday?"

"Why that would be wonderful," said Allison. "It always helps to get firsthand information."

"And Bill and I will have someone to talk to for a change!"

"I'll have to check Max's schedule, though. He works pretty irregular and unpredictable hours sometimes."

"Hey. We're not going anywhere. Whenever you can. I'll cook up a mess of jambalaya. It's shrimp, sausage and rice in Cajun sauce."

"Sounds yummy," said Allison. "Say, what did you mean by Mr. Davis needing steadier payments?"

"Oh, it's mostly a rumor, but I hear some of the people who bought lots are having trouble making the payments, and some of them are blaming Mr. Davis."

"Why would they blame him?"

"Oh, you know how people are. They make a bad decision then blame someone else for not stopping them. See, I was walking Bruno here past the sales office a few weeks ago and there was this palooka in there raising hell about how he was swindled because he wasn't able to resell his lot. The sales guy tried to explain that the prices of resales were something beyond his control, but the guy seemed to think he had a guarantee of some kind. Demanded his money back and just raised Cain."

"So how did it end?"

Nancy shook her head. "Honey, I'm not sure it did end. The guy stalked out saying that he would make them all pay one way or the other."

Chapter 12
The lake

Max and the sheriff drove south in the sheriff's Model T. They passed two tourist camps and dozens of billboards advertising Florida land for sale.

"Don't think I don't know what you were doing in Russo's office, Hurlock," Atley said when they were a few blocks away.

"Same as you. I was investigating," said Max.

"All that balloon juice about my hunch and my idea to search the other part of the office. Shoot; I didn't have any hunch like that and you know it."

"No? Well, perhaps I was mistaken."

"You were trying to show me as to how you're not a glory hunter and as to how I shouldn't worry about you showing me up. You were ready to give me credit for finding a major piece of evidence I had actually missed completely. You wanted to prove that you're willing to share the credit even if it wasn't deserved. You just wanted to gain my confidence, that's what you were doing."

Max was silent for a minute.

"So, did I succeed?"

The sheriff grinned. "Yeah, pretty much."

Max just smiled to himself.

"So Max, do you have any idea of what in the blue blazes happened at Russo's office?"

"Oh, it's Max now?"

"Well, it's too awkward calling you Hurlock. So what do you think happened in Russo's office?"

"Well, Roy G., I have an idea, but I need more evidence to flesh it out."

"And you think we'll find that evidence at Lake George?"

"I don't know, but assuming the same person committed both crimes, maybe there will be some pattern or quirk that could tell us something. Speaking of which, did your people look at the records of property buyers that bought through Russo and Godfrey?"

"Yep. There are 67 people who bought property through both Russo and Godfrey. Five have since died and most of the sixty two remaining live out of state, so sifting through them will be tough. Questioning them will be even tougher. We've asked the local police to help us screen these people."

"Sounds like a long shot," Max agreed. "How about people who have made threats?"

"There's a dozen all told, but nobody made threats to both Russo and Godfrey, so that looks like a dead end."

"How about complaints to the Chamber of Commerce or irate letters to the editor and things like that?"

"We found a few, but they were pretty mild; not the sort of thing that you would think would turn homicidal."

"All right," said Max. "I assume we will continue to narrow down the list. Now tell me about the Godfrey murder on the lake.

"Not much to tell. The upshot is that Mr. Robert Godfrey, a local real estate developer went out for a day of fishing by himself, something he did pretty much every week. He anchored at the mouth of a cove in plain sight of Ed's marina about a half mile or so away and at least a hundred yards from the nearest shore. Sometime during the day, someone got out to him and bludgeoned him to death without being seen."

Max nodded. "Sounds like the Invisible Man all right, and it seems he can now walk on water. A pretty clever fellow."

As they approached the lake, they passed an area where a dozen black men looked as if they were preparing to cut down pine trees under the hot sun. Several white supervisors were standing by on horseback. Atley frowned, but Max was curious.

"I didn't know Florida had a lumber industry."

'That's a Turpentine camp," said Atley. "Almost twenty percent of the world's Turpentine comes from Florida. They're not cutting the trees down; they're stripping some bark and cutting grooves called 'catfaces' to bleed off sap to make Turpentine."

"It looks like hot and dirty work," said Max.

"It is," said Atley. "A Turpentine camp is one step above slavery and not a very big step at that. It's a damned racket. They hire coloreds to do the work and promise them good pay, but then charge them for tools, transportation, food, and I don't know what-all. They can work for years and never get ahead of the money they wind up owing. If one of them runs away, they set the dogs on him, or the local police. They called me to track one down last year. I found him hiding in a swamp. He told me about what was going on in that camp. It was enough to turn your stomach."

"Did you bring him in?"

"No. He slipped away. They never did find him."

"Slipped away? You had an unarmed man cornered in a swamp and he slipped away? How did that happen?"

Atley looked at Max sharply. "Would *you* have dragged him back to that place?"

"No," said Max. "I don't believe I would have."

Atley nodded. "Well, just between you and me, I gave him a five dollar bill, turned away and counted to a hundred. When I turned back, he was gone. Like I said, he slipped away."

Max shook his head. "So the hard-nosed sheriff has a compassionate streak."

"And don't you be telling anybody," said Atley. "I got a reputation to keep up."

"I don't see how a sense of justice is necessarily a handicap for a lawman," said Max.

"You'd be surprised. I been a cop since I got out of high school. It's all I ever wanted to be, but I wanted to chase criminals, not victims. If that means looking the other way once in a while, well..."

Max smiled. "Roy G., I think you and I are going to get along just fine."

They arrived at Lake George a few minutes later. "Godfrey kept a small fishing boat at Ed's Marina about another mile or so along this road," said Atley. "I talked to Ed a few days ago, but you can try your luck. Ed's a little crusty."

"Crusty? What do you mean?"

Atley chuckled. "You'll see."

A twisting dirt road led to an unpainted wood shack with a weathered sign that said simply "Ed's Boats". Several piers poked out in the lake and provided a place for an assortment of small boats. From a board walkway by the shack, you could see almost the entire lake glistening in the sun. Only a few boats were visible.

"Hey, Ed," called Atley. "It's the sheriff again. You got a minute?"

A grumpy looking man in a torn shirt appeared chomping an unlit cigar.

"I got the same number of minutes as anyone else, sheriff. That's why I don't want to spend them answering damn fool questions again. I already told you everything I know."

"Ed, this is Max Hurlock. He's helping the police track down the murderer. I think it might help if you could talk to him. I know you already told me what you remember, but sometimes it helps to repeat. Sometimes it jogs your memory and helps you recall some little detail you might have missed."

Ed looked Max over critically.

"So what are you; some kinda fancy expert?"

"Do I look fancy?" Max replied. "I'm just an ordinary guy from up on the Chesapeake Bay trying to help out."

"Chesapeake Bay, huh? So I guess you must be a boat expert too."

Max shrugged. "I know a bilge strake from a taff rail."

Ed looked at the sheriff, then back to Max.

"All right. What do you want to know?"

"When you found Mr. Godfrey, he was alone and there were no other boats around. Is that right?"

"That's right."

"If some other boat had approached Mr. Godfrey during the day, do you think you would have seen it?"

"Mister. I was out on the docks all day. I'd have seen it if another boat was there. I'd have noticed it, too, because Mr. Godfrey liked his privacy. And the lake was calm that day, so even if I missed the boat, I'd have seen its wake."

"I understand Mr. Godfrey was a regular around here."

"Yep. Went out fishing every Thursday. Went to the same spot most days too."

"Where was that?"

Ed pointed northward.

"Just off that point of land over there."

"If I drew a line from here through where the boat was anchored, where would it hit the shoreline over there?"

"Oh, I'd say about where that sort of twisted oak tree is on the opposite bank."

"And you could clearly see him from here?"

"Yup. It's only maybe a half a mile away. Couldn't see him real good but I could see the boat right enough, especially with the binoculars. That's how I knew he was still there when it was getting dark. I figured maybe his outboard might be acting up, or he'd fallen asleep; he does that once in a while, so I went out to get him. Then..."

"That's sort of the mouth of a cove, isn't it?" Max asked. "What's that land behind it, where you pointed out the twisted Oak tree?"

Ed looked at the point. "Nothin' special. It's just some woods and scrub."

"Uh huh. Do you remember anyone else asking about that area in the week or two before it happened; some stranger maybe?"

"There's always a few new faces popping up around the lake. Most of 'em are looking to rent a boat, but nobody...wait a minute. About two weeks ago, there was this one fella talked about renting a boat but never did. Wanted to know about the fishing over towards the point. Strolled around and looked at the lake, then asked about the cove."

"What did you tell him?" Max asked.

"I just told him that it was a pretty good spot and that Mr. Godfrey fished there dang near every Thursday and swore by it."

"You mentioned Mr. Godfrey's name to this stranger?"

"Well, sure. Why wouldn't I?"

"No reason. Then what?"

"He asked about my rental rates then left."

"What did this fellow look like?" Atley jumped in.

"Looked like? Oh, I don't know. Like anybody I guess. About your height with brown hair. Hard to see his face very well, 'cause he wore dark glasses. He talked like he was from up north, maybe a tin canner. He didn't leave a name or anything like that."

"And you'd never seen him before?" Max asked.

"Not before and not since."

"Here's my card," said Atley. "If this guy shows up again, or you remember anything else, give me a call, all right?"

"You think he could be our boy?"Atley asked when they were back in the Model T.

"Maybe, but we need a lot more information. Are you familiar with the lake?"

"Pretty much. I used to go hunting there. Why?"

"Could you get us to that wooded area on the other side of the point?"

"Sure. There's a narrow dirt road back there somewhere, if I can find it again."

An overgrown service road led into the woods on the other side of the cove. After a few hundred yards, that road disappeared as well. Atley brought the automobile to a halt in front of a fallen tree. All was silent except for the faint buzz of insects.

Max got out and looked around.

"It looks like someone else was here within the last few weeks. There are some tire tracks, but they're too old to tell anything else.

"So someone else was here," said Atley. "Probably a hunter. Now what?"

"Now we walk. I have a compass with me."

Max consulted an Esso road map Atley had in the car and then his compass. He indicated a direction and they started out through the woods. The woods were not thick and the walking was easy. Soon they came to the shore of Lake George. From the beach area, they could see the marina in the distance.

"I think we're just about in the right place," said Max. "If I'm not mistaken, this is the twisted Oak tree Ed pointed out."

"The right place for what?"

"It looks like Godfrey was anchored maybe 70-100 yards or so offshore from where we are standing. You can also tell by the relative position of the marina."

Atley looked. "Looks like it. So what?"

"Sheriff, help me look around and see if there are any signs of someone dragging a bulky object into the woods. You know, broken branches, scrapes on the ground..."

Atley shook his head. "Max, the body was found in the boat. No one dragged it into the woods."

"I realize that. Just look, would you? I'll take this direction."

They walked up and down the narrow beach for a few minutes. Then Atley called out.

"Hey, Max. Take a look here."

Max arrived to see a broken branch on a bush and several footprints in a soft area nearby.

"Just what I thought. Let's see if we can find anything else," said Max, heading into the woods.

Atley reluctantly followed Max into the warm dampness of the woods and they found several other signs that a heavy object had been recently dragged. Presently they came to a tangled mound of broken branches and honeysuckle. Max started pulling the creepers away.

Atley pitched in and soon they had exposed what was under the mound. He stood wide eyed, wiping some sweat from his forehead.

"A canoe?"

Max nodded as he cleared branches away. "It looks like an old canvas type. A little beat up, but lightweight and serviceable."

"So the killer got to Godfrey in a canoe?"

"It looks that way. He must have paddled out acting friendly, or maybe in need of help, then smashed Godfrey over the head when his back was turned. Then he paddled back the way he came and dragged the canoe into the woods, leaving nothing behind but a dead body in a boat."

"And nobody saw him?"

"It was on a weekday, remember? During the week, the lake is pretty dead if you'll pardon the expression."

Atley wasn't convinced. "He was in plain sight of Ed at the marina, but Ed didn't see a thing. How do you explain that?"

"Let's go back to the beach and you'll see."

Max pulled the canoe forward a foot or so. "Not that heavy, but it would still be a chore to drag it here from the road."

Atley nodded. "Nothing a normal man couldn't do."

"No," said Max. "Well, let's get back to the beach."

77

A few minutes later, after trudging back through the undergrowth, they emerged at the lakeside.

"All right, Max. I can see Ed's place from here and we know Ed could see Godfrey's boat. I'll tell you what I think. I think the invisible man swam out and killed Godfrey, otherwise, Ed would have seen him. I mean, how in tarnation could the killer paddle a canoe around the lake without being seen?"

"Geometry," Max answered.

"Geometry? Max, what are you talking about?"

"But if the killer brought that canoe here from the service road, it brings up another troubling point."

"Max, I think we have enough of those already. Er...what point, exactly?"

Max picked up a stone and skipped it across the water. "If the killer was able to drag the boat here, he must have been in good physical condition. He couldn't have been suffering from any serious wound or injury. And that means..."

Atley snapped his fingers.

"That means the blood we found on the floor at the Russo place didn't belong to the killer."

Max nodded. "It also means that Russo apparently fired at the killer in that tiny office and somehow missed completely, yet managed to get someone else's blood on the floor thirty feet away."

Atley massaged is temples. "Tarnation, Max; seems like the more you find out, the less we know!"

Chapter 13
Plans

On a bright and warm Florida morning, a quiet stranger sat at a window table at the Swaying Palm coffee shop across from the Newsome Building in Orlando. He wore glasses with heavy frames and sported a thick mustache. Had anyone been observing the man closely, which no one was, they might have noticed that the glasses had plain glass lenses, and the mustache was a fake.

A few other customers populated the tables and sipped coffee and read newspapers, pretty much oblivious to their surroundings.

The man with the fake mustache took out a pocket watch and checked the time. Another five minutes to go. Everything moved about normally on the street in front of the Newsome Building, home of the J. Daniels Development Company on the fourth floor. Most of the workers had already arrived. They could be seen filtering in to the main entrance for the past half hour or so, the women wearing bright dresses and the men wearing dark suits in spite of the building Florida heat.

Most of them went in the front door on the street, but a few went in one of the two side doors that led directly to stairwells. There was no mystery about this; the employees on the higher floors invariably went in the front door to the elevator while some on the lower floors used the stairs. The man in the coffee shop took out a small, leather bound notebook and made a note.

As the man sat at a window table of the café across the street he noted the "Office space for rent" sign was still in place on a second floor window and made another note.

"Another cup of coffee?" the clerk asked.

"That would be fine. Thank you."

Another cup of coffee appeared and the man sipped it contentedly as he read the newspaper spread out on the table. Page two featured an article speculating on who killed the two real estate men. They referred to the culprit as the invisible man.

The man chuckled to himself. Invisible? No; more like hiding in plain sight. He read the rest of the article and noted that the murders were getting a lot of attention. The writer of the article included some speculation about how the killer had managed to pull off two seemingly impossible crimes; speculation that was completely wrong. The man smiled again.

A grey automobile pulled up across the street and a man got out and went in the front door of the office building. The man at the café checked his pocket watch once again. Exactly the same time every day, almost to the second. Very good.

He waited another twenty minutes, stood up, folded the paper, paid the check with a good tip, then casually walked across the street.

He walked in the front door past the man at the small desk in the lobby. The man was also reading the morning newspaper and only occasionally glanced at the dwindling number of people in the lobby.

The man noted the single elevator and was interested to see it was one of the new self-service types with no full time operator, only a lever on the inside to set the desired floor. Yes, this would do nicely.

He walked back out of the lobby and on to the street. This time the man at the desk didn't bother to look up.

Outside, the Invisible Man strolled around to the alley and opened the door leading to a stairwell. He listened for a moment, then walked up one floor and tried the door to the office.

The door was unlocked.

Inside, the vacant office covered the entire second floor. The invisible man looked around casually, then made some more notes in his book and snapped it shut. Smiling with satisfaction, the Invisible Man walked back down the stairs, through the door into the alley and was gone.

John Reisinger

Chapter 14
Crackers

Allison caught the boat back to St Augustine around four and spent a while strolling some of the old streets near the hotel.

The glare of the sun was hot and Allison started looking around for a place that afforded some shade. On a street several blocks from the hotel she saw a dusty looking medicine shop with some bottles, crutches and assorted medical supplies in the window. They had apparently been here a long time.

Allison pushed open the front door and heard a tinny bell announce her presence. The place was gloomy, but clean. A soda fountain ran along one wall and two customers sat sipping some sort of foamy drinks. An ancient overhead fan tuned slowly, clicking with each revolution. On the other side was a pharmacist's cage and an elderly man sat watching her.

"Good afternoon, Miss. Can I help you with anything?"

The man looked friendly enough, so Allison replied.

"I'm Allison Hurlock and I'm writing a magazine article about Florida."

The man suddenly looked a little less friendly. He shrugged.

"Well, it's right outside," he said. "You can't miss it."

Allison smiled and the man softened a little. (Men usually did when Allison smiled at them.)

"I can see that Florida any time. I mean the Florida of people who have lived here for years. The Florida beyond the slick development and beaches. The real Florida."

The man hesitated, then spoke to a couple seated at the end of the counter sipping Coca Colas.

"Say, Ben. This lady wants to know about cracker country."

The couple looked up curiously. They were tanned and wiry looking, as if they had been somehow carved out of an old Hickory stump. Their clothes were clean but worn and had been patched several times.

"Ben here is a third generation cracker. Molly's people go back before that. They're the real old time Florida. They live in the backwoods, but they come into town for supplies several times a year and Ben always treats the Mrs. to a phosphate at the soda fountain here."

Allison was confused. "A cracker? What is that?"

Ben spoke in a gravelly voice with a thick southern accent.

"Tarnation, young lady. A cracker's just a homesteading farmer. Crackers come here from Georgia or the Carolinas after the War Between the States looking for a new home. They settle empty land in the interior and even the Everglades. We raise cattle and do some faming. We don't ask for nothin' and don't cotton to outsiders tellin' us what to do."

Allison nodded. "I see. Are there a lot of these 'crackers' around?"

Ben scratched his neck in contemplation. "Hard to say. They're pretty much scattered around the whole state what with the farmin' and all."

"They don't live in towns?" Allison asked.

"Not towns like St Augustine, but there are some smaller places where you'll find crackers, places that ain't on no map, places like Hog Valley, Yankeetown, Scrambletown, and Yeehaw Junction."

"Uh, where are these places?"

"Inland a piece. We ain't partial to company most days. We just keep to ourselves, raise our cattle and get on with life."

Ben took a long pull at his phosphate. His wife stared straight ahead, demurely sipping hers through a straw.

"See," Ben continued, "we raise cattle just like they do in Texas. We let 'em roam around and graze, then round them up for market. Some of us are pretty good cattle wranglers."

"Cattle ranching in the wilds of Florida," said Allison. "You learn something new every day. So what do you think about all the people from up north coming to Florida to buy land or to build?"

Ben snorted in derision. "Hell, most of 'em couldn't find a coconut on a palm tree, but it's them real estate people I blame. If they stay near the coast mostly, it don't really bother us none, but some of 'em are startin' to get greedy like. They buy up big tracts farther inland where they're cheap, then cut 'em up in to little building lots and sell 'em to northerners what don't know no better. If they keep pushin' and pushin', pretty soon they'll be eatin' up grazing land some crackers use for their cattle. I'll tell you, if they keep spreadin' out the way they been doin', they'll start getting' too close for comfort. The crackers ain't gonna like it one bit."

Allison suddenly felt a chill in the muggy air.

"What will happen then?" Allison asked.

Ben put his glass down with a clatter. "I'll tell you what'll happen then, young lady; there's going to be trouble."

Chapter 15
Clues

That night, Max and Allison ate at a small café near the fort. The waiter served up a platter of Jambalaya that made Allison wish she was a better cook.

"Look at this; it has rice, chicken, tomatoes, sausage, shrimp...Who would have thought that throwing all this stuff together could taste so good?" Max exclaimed.

"It must be the climate," said Allison. She took a bite. "Oh, my. That is wonderful."

For a minute, they both ate in contented silence, then Allison spoke up.

"How are you and the sheriff getting along? Does he resent your involvement?"

"He was a little wary of me at first, but I think he's so desperate for help, he's learning to live with the idea. Atley is a good lawman, and he's no fool, but I think he's in a bit over his head on this one. He's more used to arresting drunks and poachers. Multiple well-planned murders are not his usual bill of fare. Of course, I'm not exactly walking on water myself. But enough about my troubles, did you get any good article material today?"

"I think so. I went to Davis Shores and talked to a woman who invited us for dinner. She promised to serve Jambalaya, in fact. They just built a house there. Then I talked to a genuine Florida Cracker."

"You talked to a cracker? It must have been lunch time."

"Not the food item, Max, one of the old time Florida residents. Sort of salt water cowboys who raise cattle in the interior."

"Are you a magazine writer or an anthropologist?"

"The funny thing is that I'm not really investigating the murders, but I turned up two more suspects."

"That's two more than I have. So spill it; who are they?"

Allison told him about the angry property buyer at Davis Shores and the warning from Ben about trouble if real estate sales started getting too close to cracker territory.

"Good work," said Max. "At this point I don't have anything better. I'm still looking for someone who is killing off real estate people one by one in a spectacular way, but I still don't know why, let alone who."

"So you think the two murders were by the same man?"

"I think so, but it's early yet and I am open to new evidence. It seems to me that the killer is intentionally making the murders as mysterious as possible."

"So why would he want to do that?"

"Oh, I can think of several reasons. If the police can't figure out how the crimes were done, they'll have a hard time figuring out who did them. What's more, even if they do find the killer, they'll have the devil's own time getting a conviction in court if they can't explain how the crimes were committed. A defense attorney would have a bucket full of reasonable doubt to work with."

"That's true," said Allison, "and I can think of another reason."

"What's that?"

"Maybe it's his way of thumbing his nose at the authorities he has a grudge against and also a way of assuring he'll make a big splash in the papers."

"That's a good point," said Max, "and it's just the sort of thing an unhappy investor might do to call attention to his grievance. So maybe that's the killer's motive after all."

"And this one man somehow committed both murders without being seen and without leaving a clue as to how he did it? Wouldn't he have to somehow know a lot about his victims to pull that off? He'd have to know their routine, where they go each day, and their comings and goings."

"Of course," said Max. "Our killer presumably travels around Florida at his leisure picking out victims and studying their habits for some period before he strikes," said Max.

"I suppose that's the only way he could do it," said Allison.

"So it would seem, but who has the time, money and freedom to spend months traveling around watching people, forming a plan and then murdering them?"

Allison frowned in thought. "Someone without a regular job, maybe? Someone who is wealthy? Or maybe a traveling salesman or a company field rep of some sort. That would give him the freedom and the excuse to travel around the state on his own without anyone smelling a rat."

Max nodded slowly. "Yes, possibly, but that brings up another problem."

"Such as?"

"Such as the police theory of the case. Everyone thinks the killer is a disgruntled investor who lost his shirt buying now-worthless Florida land. The murders are his revenge for his financial ruin."

"Considering the way the murders were done, that seems like a reasonable motive," Allison remarked.

"Oh, the motive is certainly reasonable enough," said Max, "but if our killer lost his savings in bad real estate deals, how can he have the time and money to travel around Florida for months on end the way he seems to be doing?"

"Max, that's right. He obviously doesn't work at a traditional job, but has some substantial financial resources, so the theory of an angry and desperate man who is broke because of the real estate industry has some problems."

"Of course, that doesn't get us any closer, but it's a factor to consider. If the killer isn't an angry real estate investor, who is he, and what's his motive?"

"Well, I don't envy you, Max. Getting to the bottom of this mess is going to be tough. On one hand, the sort of person who would be most likely to do this wouldn't have the resources, but someone who has the ability and the resources wouldn't have the motive. I suppose that's why they call these things mysteries. Anyway, Glenn Curtiss and I have faith that you will find out."

"I hope you're right," Max sighed. "Somewhere there's a logical explanation that fits all the facts, even the contradictory ones. I just have to slog along until I find it, I guess. It's a frustrating case. But do you know what the worst part is?"

"What?"

"The worst part is that I have a feeling the killer is just getting started."

Chapter 16
Death between floors

At the Newsome Building in Orlando, the nervous clerk looked at the wall clock in the Daniels Real Estate office on the fourth floor.

"It's almost time. Mr. Daniels will be here in five minutes. Everyone, look sharp."

The office continued its usual last minute turmoil. After all, Mr. Daniels arrived at nine each morning and expected to see everything in perfect order. Each day the elevator door would open and Mr. Daniels would pass down the rows of desks with a drill sergeant's eye.

Fred, the desk clerk in the lobby, kept an eye out for Mr. Daniels as well, and discretely phoned up to the fifth floor each day to let them know he was on his way, just so no one got taken by surprise. Of course, the call was hardly necessary, since Mr. Daniels arrived at almost the same time every day. Today was no different as he saw the form of Mr. Daniels appear at the front door of the building at the usual time.

"Good morning Mr. Daniels."

Daniels didn't look up from the newspaper he was reading as he walked.

"Morning, Fred," he said briskly.

Fred noted the time and placed his morning call to the fourth floor as Mr. Daniels made his way to the open elevator door.

"He's here," Fred whispered. "He's almost at the elevator." A few seconds later, Mr. Daniels entered the elevator, which, as usual for this time of day, had no other passengers. The elevator was one of the new automatic kinds that do not require an operator. Mr. Daniels appreciated that feature, since it meant there was one fewer person he would have to exchange pleasantries with each day. Nothing was more boring to Mr. Daniels then to be trapped in an elevator with someone who felt compelled to tell his entire life story to the first stranger he encountered.

Mr. Daniels looked at his watch; right on time. He pressed the button for the floor and watched as the doors closed.

On the fourth floor everyone was taking their places, like actors preparing for the curtain to go up on the first act. No one wanted to be the subject of Mr. Daniels's attentions when he first arrived because that was when he was at his grumpiest and was most likely to dress someone down in front of everyone else. Once he got to his office, everyone knew, he mellowed somewhat and people could breathe easier. So papers rustled, typewriters chattered, and generally, noses were pressed against grindstones. One office wit cracked that more work was done in the few minutes waiting for Mr. Daniels to arrive in the morning than was done the rest of the day. It was something of an exaggeration, but not much.

So when the bell rang and the doors to the elevator opened, no one dared look up until they heard the gruff "Morning everyone" from Mr. Daniels.

But the greeting never came. No one spoke or looked up for several seconds until finally, one brave soul stole a glance at the open elevator.

"Oh, my God!" he sputtered. "Something's happened to Mr. Daniels!"

Every other head in the office rose and turned towards the elevator. There, crumpled in the corner of the cab was the lifeless body of Mr. Daniels, still clutching a wet red spot on his chest.

John Reisinger

Chapter 17
The third murder

Max stopped by the Sheriff's office first thing to see if there was any word on the investigation into the disgruntled customers of the two murdered men.

"We asked police in other states to question the ones on our list of unhappy property buyers, but nothing has turned up yet."

"Have they been able to eliminate anyone?" Max asked.

"Yeah, eight of our suspects have alibies for one or both of the murders. I have a few undercover cops making the rounds to the local speakeasies to see what they can pick up. I just got a report from our man in St Augustine. He was at the Zorayda last night and heard some pretty interesting gossip from one of the staff there. It seems some guy was in there complaining about real estate developers."

"The Zorayda?"

"AKA the Zorayda Club. It's a smaller version of a Moorish palace in Spain, lots of pointed arches, tile work and fountains. It started out as a private residence, but now it's a speakeasy and gambling place."

"Doesn't sound like much of a secret," Max remarked. "If you know about the place, why don't the Prohibition police shut it down?"

"Oh, the place is too well connected; too much risk of arresting the wrong people. You can't swing a cat in the place without hitting a local judge or politician. Besides, the Zorayda is an institution around here."

Max shook his head. "Sounds like the whole town is an institution," he muttered.

A secretary called from across the room. "Sheriff, there's a phone call for you. It's the constable down in Ordando. He asked if you were heading up the Invisible Man investigation, then asked to speak with you. He said it was urgent."

Atley sighed. "Orlando? Don't know what could be so danged urgent down there; it's nothing but orange groves and swamps. Well, I guess I should see what he wants."

Atley picked up the candlestick phone on his desk and held the receiver up to his ear.

"Atley here... What's that?... Are you sure? And there was nobody else there? Where?" Atley grabbed a pencil and a map. "Where is it? I see the place. Now look. Do me a favor, would you? I have Max Hurlock here. He's something of an expert on this sort of thing and he's helping out. I'd like to come down and bring him along. We'll be there this afternoon, but I need you to guard the crime scene and keep things as quiet as possible. Seal of the entire building and don't let anyone leave. I know the medical examiner will have to take the body away for sanitary reasons, so have someone take plenty of photographs of it first. See you then."

Atley hung up the phone and stood up in one motion.

"Grab your hat, Max. The Zorayda Club will have to wait. The Invisible Man has struck again."

They were out the door in a few seconds.

"The victim is Jerome Daniels of J. Daniels Property Development in Orlando. He's a big developer and sells plenty of building lots."

"It fits the pattern of victims," Max agreed. "So how was he killed...another impossible crime?"

"The most impossible so far," said Atley. "He was shot to death in an elevator somewhere between the first and fourth floor. He was seen entering the empty elevator on the first floor and his office staff saw the body when the elevator arrived at his fourth floor office a minute later.'

Max nodded. "An impressive bit of work, and a problem worthy of our attention."

"Yeah. Our killer seems to be trying to outdo himself. That's good in a way. Maybe he'll spend so much effort on being clever he'll slip up somewhere else and we'll get him."

"Of course, he could leave a lot of bodies in his wake by then," said Max. "Anyway, I wouldn't count on any big slipups from this guy. He strikes me as careful and meticulous."

"You think so?"

"Absolutely. He's on murder number three and we still have no witnesses. He isn't leaving much of a trace. And then there is the matter of the notes."

"Notes? What notes? He didn't leave any notes."

"Exactly," said Max. "Look; this guy has killed three people in ways guaranteed to attract attention. Killers who do that usually send letters to the police or to newspapers, letters bragging, taunting, or justifying what they are doing. Often, the letters will reveal clues about the killer, but there have been no letters, so our killer is cautious and covering his tracks, even though his crimes border on the spectacular. I'd say he has remarkable self-control as well. People who commit sensational; crimes usually crave notoriety and can't resist crowing about it, but not this guy."

"Great," said Atley, "an anonymous showoff."

"How do you suppose he's picking his victims?" Max said, finally.

Atley shrugged. "He's obviously picking people in Florida real estate development or sales."

"Sure," said Max, "but where is he finding them?"

"What do you mean?"

"Look, you're a lifelong Florida resident and a lawman besides. Could *you* name Florida's leading real estate people?"

"What are you getting at?"

"If the killer is a disgruntled out of state investor, how is he finding these people? They aren't exactly movie stars or celebrities. Oh, he'd know the name of whomever he was dealing with, but he couldn't have bought property from all three people. How did he find the others?"

"I don't know how he finds them," said Atley, "but I know how he leaves them."

The Newsome Building was easy to find. The red brick building was the tallest on the block and the only one with a police officer guarding the front door. The local constable, Donald Billings, met them at the front door, along with a shorted man who looked like a security guard.

"You guys got here fast. Good. We have a real head scratcher on our hands."

"Not to mention a mixed metaphor," Max murmured.

"This is Fred. He's sort of the doorman and receptionist around here. Tell them what you saw, Fred."

"I saw Mr. Daniels get in the elevator at eight thirty, just the way he always did, and he was alone. I'll swear to it on a stack of bibles."

"Was anyone else around?" Atley asked.

"No sir. Other than Mr. Daniels and me, the lobby was empty. Everyone else gets here at eight sharp."

Max, meanwhile, was walking towards the elevator. Atley followed. The elevator was an ordinary Otis model, a type without an operator. The body had been removed, but a puddle of blood remained.

Constable Billings looked over their shoulders. "He got in the elevator alone and was alone when it reached the fourth floor, only he was shot to death. Nobody saw anything and nobody heard anything."

"Could the elevator have stopped at another floor before it went to Daniels's office?" Atley asked.

"No way," said Billings, shaking his head. "I checked. The elevator is controlled from the inside once the rider specifies a floor. The elevator won't stop anywhere else until it completes the first request, or gets another request from inside the cab itself. If anyone wanted to make the cab stop anywhere else, he'd have to be *inside* the cab and no one else was."

"Could someone have tampered with the elevator to make it stop at another floor?" Atley asked.

Billings shook his head. "The man from the Otis elevator company just left. He checked out the controls and the switch mechanism. They were working perfectly with no sign of tampering."

Atley looked at the paneling in the elevator. "No sign of any opening or sliding hatchway or anything like that. What do you think, Max?"

Max was looking at the floor. "This blood is at the front, right by the door," Max observed.

"That's where the body was found."

"What's on the second and third floor?" Max asked.

"The second floor is vacant. There's a For Rent sign out front. The third floor is part of the Daniels Company, but there were four people in sight of the elevator doors and they all swear the elevator didn't stop there."

"Sheriff, I'm going to take a look at the other floors," said Max.

Max wandered off and inspected the stairwells, then climbed the stairs to the second floor. He pushed open the door to the second floor and observed a mostly empty space. He walked in slowly, looking at the floor, until he came to the elevator doors. He looked around a few minutes, then went to the fourth floor.

On the top floor, the employees of J. Daniels were officially still at work, but most people seemed to be huddled in little groups whispering nervously. Billings and Atley were already there.

"This is Doris, Mr. Daniels's secretary," said Billings, indicating a thin, middle aged woman holding a handkerchief to her face. Doris told the same story everyone else had. Finally Max spoke up.

"Do you keep a phone log, Miss Doris?"

She seemed surprised by the question. "A phone log? Why, yes."

"Could you look through Mr. Daniels's calls for the last two weeks and see if here are any names you don't recognize; especially an unrecognized name that only shows up once?" Max smiled his most ingratiating smile.

"Why...yes; of course."

"Thank you. Would you please let Mr. Atley know the result when you have it? He'll give you his card."

"I'll have the local police send us copies of the crime scene photographs when they're developed."

Max nodded. "That's fine. I would suggest they check with local hardware stores and gun shops to see if anyone has bought a pistol silencer in the last week or so."

Later, when they were headed back to St Augustine, Max was lost in thought. Atley finally piped up. "Come on, Max. What do you think?"

"Think?"

"Yes, how did the Invisible Man pull this one off?"

"Sorry, I was just thinking about something."

"Such as?"

"Well, our killer goes to a lot of trouble to make his crimes baffling. That way he gets the attention he seeks, but also make solving the case harder. That's a clever move if you think about it. See, most things that make a case attention getting, such as a crime with some weird flourish, some very unusual circumstances, or some peculiar weapon would also make the case easier to solve, since it might draw the attention of someone who recognizes some aspect that points to the murderer. Our man, however, is too clever to fall into that trap. By making each crime baffling and using fairly simple and untraceable ways of doing it, our killer creates so much confusion and mystery, he generates attention while making the case *harder* to solve. It's a good trick. You have to hand it to him."

"You mean you know how he pulled off the elevator murder? How about letting me in on it?"

"I suspect, but I don't really know. I need another piece of evidence first. We should have it pretty soon. Meanwhile, I suggest we stop by that roadside barbeque shack we passed on the way down for a bite of dinner. If they have a phone, I'd like to call Allison and tell her where I am."

Cooper's Down Home Southern Barbeque was the sort of place you smelled long before you actually saw it. Cooper's featured rough wooden tables with bottles of various sauces and lots of napkins. Max ordered the pulled pork, then went to the crank phone in the back to call Allison. After several efforts and a lot of static, he got through.

"Max, where are you?"

"I'll on the way back from Orlando. I was..."

"You know there's been another murder, don't you? A guy shot in an elevator."

"The story's out already? Well, I didn't think they could keep the lid on something like that. How did you hear about it?"

"I heard about it from Glenn Curtiss, when he called looking for you and sounding like a man who couldn't take much more."

"He was really upset?"

"Well, you're the detective, but that was my deduction, especially when he said 'I'm really upset.'".

Max sighed. "All right. I'll give him a call right now. I should be back around eight or so."

"Fine. I'll be waiting for you. Look out for alligators on the way back."

Max placed a second call, this time to Miami Springs. Glenn Curtiss came on the line.

"Max; what's going on? Is this Invisible Man going to wipe out every developer in Florida?"

"He's smart and he's cautious, I'm afraid. That's a bad combination from our point of view."

"And now he can kill a man in an elevator without being seen?"

"That seems to have been the case. I have an idea how he did it, but the real question is who is he? The police are still interviewing investors and running down lists of property buyers and people who have complained about unfair treatment. They haven't come up with a likely name yet, but they have eliminated a number of them."

"That would be just dandy except that the Invisible Man is doing the same thing to the developers! Look, Max; I have confidence in you and your abilities, but this thing is gaining steam. The papers will be in a frenzy about this. I'm already getting reports of developers talking about hiring bodyguards and customers afraid to go to a property office. If there's another killing, it'll be hysteria around here. This is poison. You've got to stop it!"

"I'm doing my best, Glenn. I'm as frustrated as anyone else, but we do have a few irons in the fire. I'm still following up on some thoughts."

"All right, Max. You keep at it, and don't talk to reporters. I don't want the killer to get tipped off by something he reads in the Miami Herald. I don't even want the killer to know you exist."

Max hung up the phone and rubbed his temples.

When a gloomy Max rejoined Atley at the battered wooden table, their order had arrived. Max loved pulled pork, and this version was about as good as any he had ever tasted, but he just picked at it.

For some reason, he had lost his appetite.

John Reisinger

Chapter 18
The canoe

Allison was waiting in the lobby when Atley dropped Max off around eight. They went up to the room in silence and closed the door behind them. Allison sat down on the bed and gazed at him sympathetically.

"You don't look like you're up for the baby project tonight, Max; what happened?"

Max recounted the trip to Orlando and the latest murder.

"So now the result of Glenn Curtiss hiring me is no arrest and another murder. What's more, the killer is managing to be sensational without leaving any clues."

"Max, you know how things always look bad until you come up with some answers. You'll get to the bottom of it; you always have before."

Max shook his head. "This is different, Allison. In most cases I can take my time checking clues, questioning people, and slowly build a case. There's no rush and no real limit on what I can try. But this case is different. There have been three murders so far, and no sign of a letup. Every day that passes while I'm trying to investigate means another person could be killed. Usually justice depends on my decisions, now lives do. It's terrible pressure."

Allison nodded and grasped his hand.

"It's like that time we were flying Gypsy and the engine conked out," he continued. "I could glide down and land in a field while I checked out what was wrong and fix it. This case is like trying to fix that engine while over the ocean while each second we're getting lower. That's the problem with this case; too much keeps happening and there's not a field to land in while I take stock. I just keep going down."

"Max, this isn't like you. I'm supposed to be the emotional one around here. You're the one with the cool and analytical mind, remember?"

Max flopped down next to her on the bed and rubbed his eyes. "Yeah, well, maybe I'm just tired, but it seems like there's too many loose ends to ever bring them together. Three murders; three victims, three places, and three impossible methods."

Allison was quiet for a moment.

"I was reading Today's Campus Magazine yesterday," she began. Max looked at her in confusion.

"Are you planning on a return to Goucher?" he asked.

"I try to read a wide variety of magazines to get an idea of what's selling as far as articles are concerned. Anyway, they had an article on Notre Dame's football team. You know; the Fighting Irish?"

"Uh, yes. I *have* heard of them." Max tried not to sound too sarcastic.

"They interviewed Knute Rockne, the coach, and he talked about the team spirit; you know; the usual things."

"Rah, rah."

"Yes. Anyway, Rockne said that one thing he drills into his players is to resist being distracted by the crowd noise. Some of these players are just out of high school and tend to get distracted and rattled by the tremendous din of a college game. He tells them to force themselves to concentrate on the task at hand and push the noise aside."

"I have a feeling you're trying to tell me something," said Max.

"This case is just like the others," said Allison. "The killer has a name, has a motive, and leaves clues behind. Your job is to do what you've done before and put it all together. You can do it and you can do it better than anyone else. The only thing different about this case is the amount of noise, and the fact that Glenn Curtiss, a man you admire, is part of it, but that wouldn't distract Knute Rockne and it shouldn't distract you."

Max smiled. "I don't know what it is, but suddenly I have the urge to tackle somebody."

"I thought you'd never ask."

The next morning, Max contacted Atley.

"Have we heard anything more from Orlando?"

"Have you seen the papers?"

"Not yet, but I know the word is out about the elevator murder."

"It's all over the papers on page one. They're calling our killer the Invisible Man: The King of Impossible Crimes. That's not going to make our job any easier. As for Orlando, I haven't heard anything, but with all the damned reporters that keep calling here, they'd have a hard time getting through. The press has been nipping at my heels all morning. They want a statement. Are you coming by today?"

"Maybe later," said Max. "I have to check something first."

"Oh, by the way. I got a call from Hal Chester, the office manager in the Russo locked office case. He checked with the cleaning company and tracked down the guy that cleaned up the place after the murder. He says he wiped down the key and the door handle on the inside because they both had smears of blood on them."

"Good," said Max. "That's what I thought."

"And this means what, exactly?"

"I'll tell you later."

Max set out for the local library to look at the newspapers for the past several weeks. The librarian was helpful and directed him to a dark corner by the card catalog. Max neatly stacked the newspapers and took out a pencil and a notepad. Instead of looking at the news, however, Max began scanning the for sale ads. In about an hour, he had a list the names and phone numbers of everyone who advertised a canoe for sale within 50 miles of Lake George, a total of 14 people.

At police headquarters, Max had access to the telephone in the interrogation room, so he greeted Atley, then started making calls. His method was simple; anyone who said the canoe was still for sale was given a polite thank you, but anyone who said the canoe had been sold was asked when it was sold. Any sold after the murder on the lake were eliminated. Any time Max found a canoe had been sold before the murder on the lake, he asked for more information on the canoe, then more information on the buyer if the type of canoe seemed right, and most people were glad to provide it.

At first, the calls were mundane. The average Florida canoe buyer seemed to be an obvious hunter or outdoorsman who lived nearby. Finally, Max had worked his way through all of the advertisements with telephone numbers and noted that there were still three that had only the address of the seller, since many people still didn't have telephones in their homes.

Just then, Atley opened the door and stuck his head in the interrogation room.

"I just got a call from that Doris at the J. Daniels office in Orlando where the elevator murder happened. She went through all the telephone logs for the past three weeks and found that the victim got a call from a Mr. Morrison. He didn't say what he wanted and insisted on talking to Mr. Daniels personally. Daniels talked to him for about five minutes. The thing that was odd was that there was no record of any other calls or contact with anybody by that name."

Max nodded, but said nothing.

"Well? What do you make of that information, Max? Do you think this Morrisson is the Invisible Man?"

"That's what I suspect," said Max, cautiously, "though I doubt that's his real name."

"What? Are you seriously saying that he called up his potential victim out of the blue to have a little chat?"

"Max nodded. "In a manner of speaking, yes. It was necessary to his plan."

"And what was his plan?"

"His plan was to kill Daniels in that elevator, and he succeeded."

"But what..."

"Look, I've got some theories, but I need more information. How is the investigation of the disgruntled investors going?"

"All right, Max. I suppose you know what you're doing," said Atley. "I got an update just a few minutes ago, as a matter of fact."

"Good."

"They've eliminated the people that have died, and they've been working their way through the rest.

They've checked out the whereabouts of the remaining people and found that all but three had a good alibi for at least one of the crimes."

"Were they able to track down everyone on the list?"

"Not yet. Two are traveling abroad, two have moved, and two just didn't respond when an investigator knocked on their door. I expect we'll catch up with them soon enough."

Max sighed. "Too many loose ends. Well, I have to take a ride this afternoon."

"Need any help?"

"No. This is a long shot and there's no sense having two people on the same wild goose chase. I'm going to try to find out where our man got the canoe he used in the Lake George murder. If I can track it down, maybe I can get a description of the killer."

"It's worth a try," said Atley, "but it seems like a long shot."

Allison screwed the top back on her pen and sat back in her chair at the Hotel Alcazar's sidewalk café. She took a sip of her coffee and looked over what she had just written.

Florida: It's not what you think
The hidden sides of the Sunshine State
By Allison Hurlock

Florida is the place everybody thinks they know. Everyone has seen the movies, or the magazine articles, or the advertisements. Many people have even bought property in the Sunshine State, so it's not surprising that Florida seems as familiar as a glass of orange juice. It's all palm trees, beaches, balmy weather and maybe the occasional hurricane.

But Florida has hidden depths that never seem to show up on the travel posters and remain invisible to the casual visitor, and even to many longtime residents.

"Not bad. I think this is a pretty good angle. It's different without being sensational. Just the sort of thing the magazines like."

"I'm sorry. Were you talking to me?"

Allison turned around and saw a smiling man at the next table addressing her. He was wearing a white linen suit and a Panama hat.

Allison blushed slightly. She really needed to work on resisting her tendency to say things out loud.

"Oh, no. I was just talking to myself."

"Then I really am sorry," the man said, removing his hat to reveal immaculately groomed blond hair.

"Well..."

"Please excuse my curiosity, but I happen to take a great interest in the world around me and I noticed you were writing just now. Are you a novelist?"

Allison resisted her urge to politely demur and decided to see if this man might produce something she could use in the article.

"I'm a magazine writer. I'm just starting another article."

"You write magazine articles? What a coincidence; I *read* magazine articles!"

Allison stifled a smile.

"I may have read some of your articles. May I ask your name?"

"Allison Hurlock...*Mrs.* Allison Hurlock."

The "Mrs." Didn't seem to dampen the stranger's enthusiasm. Allison Hurlock...yes, that does sound familiar. I'm sure I've read you."

And I think I can read you, Allison thought to herself.

"My name is Julian DeKuyper and I'm proud to meet you."

"Hello, Mr. DeKuyper. Are you visiting St Augustine?"

"Please call me Julian. Say; may I sit at your table? It's so awkward talking this way."

Allison shrugged. "If you'd like."

DeKuyper slid into a vacant sea at Allison's table. "Thank you. I do so hate to have my coffee alone."

"I believe I asked if you were a visitor...Julian."

"Oh, of course. Forgive me. I am a proud citizen of St Augustine, at least I have been since last year. I just love the climate, especially when everyone up north is shoveling snow."

"And how do you find the people in Florida, Julian?"

"Wonderful. They're friendly and outgoing for the most part. I am very content. So tell me about your article."

"I'm writing on the hidden side of Florida; the part the tourists never see."

"Oh, what a marvelous idea. I can't wait to read it. If you're interested in the hidden side of Florida, you must go to The Zorayda Club. It's just up the street a block or two. It was built as a private home and it's modeled after the Alhambra in Spain. It's all pointed arches, soft velvet pillows, and arabesque decorations. And the people that go there! Believe me, no article on the hidden side of Florida would be complete without a trip to the Zorayda Club. If I am not being too forward,

Allison, I would be honored to escort you there this evening in the interests of helping with your research. I'm a regular."

"You're part of the local color, then?"

"Oh, on any given night, I'm one of the least colorful characters there, believe me. So what do you say?"

"I have plans to go there with my husband and he doesn't let me date. He's old-fashioned that way."

"Allison, my intentions are honorable and entirely harmless, I assure you."

"What a relief."

"I am a patron of the arts and literature, and I admit I enjoy the company of beautiful and interesting woman such as yourself. I hope you understand."

"Yes; I think I do,' said Allison dryly. "I really must run. It was nice talking to you, Julian."

He leapt to his feet. "Now Allison, you must give me a chance. I know a lot about Florida and it could help your article."

"I don't think..."

"Here's my card. Feel free to contact me at any time if you change your mind or have any questions about Florida. We will see each other again. I promise."

Max sat in the Packard and crossed another name off his list of people who advertised canoes for sale without telephone numbers. He had not been at all surprised to find that every person on the list so far had failed to sell their canoe. Well, no wonder. Who would drive out in the swamps to buy a canoe sight unseen? He had one more name left on the list. Well, he knew it was a longshot.

He arrived at the last address, an unpainted wood shack in the backwoods in the afternoon and was walking towards the front door when a man appeared and greeted him.

"Good afternoon," said Max, holding a copy of the newspaper with the want ad. "My name is Max. I understand you have a canoe for sale."

"Pleased to meet you. Name's Carl. Sorry; that canoe's sold. Fella came by here maybe two weeks ago and paid cash on the spot."

"You don't say. Did he say what he wanted it for?"

Carl shrugged. "It's a canoe. There's only so many things you *can* do with it."

Max laughed "Good point. Well, I suppose he was a fisherman or a tourist."

"Didn't say, but he wasn't from around here. Kind of an odd duck, if you ask me."

"Odd? What do you mean?"

"Well, he was wearing dark glasses and a big hat, even though the trees make it shady around here most of the time. And he had a mustache that I thought was phony, 'cause it wasn't the same shade of brown as the rest of his hair. Didn't say much, neither. Acted as if he was a spy or something."

Max nodded. "That does sound unusual. Was he a tall man?"

"Maybe your height and build; nothing unusual there, but what really made me wonder was the license plate on his automobile."

Max tried to hold back his excitement. "You saw his license plate?"

"I helped him load the canoe on the roof, so I got a good look."

"I don't suppose you remember the number? I might like to look this man up and see if he'd resell that canoe."

The man shook his head. "Mister, I couldn't even tell you what *state* it was from. The plate was covered with mud."

"Oh. I guess he drove through some muddy areas to get here."

"That's what was so peculiar," said Carl, scratching his head slowly. "The rest of the automobile was clean. It was a grey Chevrolet. I mean, how does a man manage to get mud on the plate and nowheres else?"

By putting it there intentionally, Max thought.

"Well, there was one thing," the man continued. "The mud was mostly dried and a piece had fallen off right near the bottom, underneath the numbers. I could just make out the first letter V where it says the name of the state, so I figured he must have come from Virginia."

"Thank you Carl; you would make a great detective."

When Max arrived back at the sheriff's office, Atley was skeptical.

"So some guy from out of state buys a canoe and you think it was the one we found in the woods?"

"Yes, and I think Mr. Carl could identify it in a courtroom, tying the buyer with the Godfrey murder on the lake."

"And he bought a canoe from someone who remembers him and he used his personal automobile? I thought this guy was careful."

"That *is* careful. Think about his options. If he had rented a canoe, there would be a record, so that was out. If he stole a canoe, someone would have reported it and the police would be on the lookout, so that was out, but buying a canoe from someone in the backwoods and paying cash was the safest way. As for an automobile, renting a car leaves another record someone could check, but driving an out of state car in a place that is full of people from out of state is good camouflage. And just in case the canoe seller was observant, the Invisible Man slapped some mud on his license plates."

"All right, Max. So our man is from either Virginia or Vermont. That should narrow the search."

"Do we have anybody like that among the people we're investigating?"

"Well, let me check." Atley rustled some papers. "Among the ones without alibis, there are none from Vermont, but four from Virginia. Here they are:

Ronald Anderson: He bought three high end waterfront lots to the tune of about three grand, but couldn't resell them and the monthly payments keep coming due. We couldn't contact him, but his wife says he's a traveling salesman and he's often gone for months at a time, and get this- Florida is part of his territory."

"He'd have a good opportunity with the traveling salesman routine," said Max. "Who else?"

"Mario Carpellini: He only has one lot that he paid $350 for in monthly instalments he couldn't afford. That may not sound like much, but Carpellini's in the Navy, on the Pennslvania, so that's a lot of money for him. He went AWOL about the time the murders started and hasn't been heard from since."

"Hmmm. It's not conclusive, but it's certainly suspicious. Who's next?"

"Ryan Summers: He has four lots mortgaged up the hilt. He and his wife left their apartment about a month before the first murder. They were three months behind in their rent and didn't leave a forwarding address."

"Has anyone checked with relatives?" Max asked.

"We're trying. The trouble is, Summers is a common name and we don't know his wife's name. The property he bought was in his name only and he gave the now abandoned apartment as his address. The landlord doesn't have any information on him, since they didn't have a lease. Can you beat that?"

"Well, maybe he'll turn up. They'll have to keep nosing around. There's one more?"

"Yes. Sean McGuiness. He claims to be some sort of business consultant, but we're pretty sure he's really a bootlegger. As a result, he has a rather irregular schedule. His wife claims he's currently away on one of his business trips, but she's learned not to ask too many questions. She says he pretty much comes and goes as the "clients" demand. She has no idea when he'll return."

"An interesting assortment," Max remarked. "Any thoughts?"

Atley rocked back on his chair as if he were about to tell a tale in front of a pot-bellied stove. "Well, if I had to choose, I really couldn't at this point, although I think Carpellini is probably not our man. I don't think he'd have the resources to travel around planning murders, what with his Navy paycheck cut off."

Max nodded. Maybe not, but one of these people does and we've got find him."

Atley left the room to return the report. Max thought for a moment, then picked up the telephone.

John Reisinger

Chapter 19
Heads together

After dinner that night, Max and Allison strolled by Matanzas Bay near the nearly completed Bridge of Lions connecting St Augustine to Davis Shores.

"Once the bridge gets finished, I think things might pick up for D.P. Davis and Davis Shores," said Max. "It's a beautiful area."

"I'm afraid it will take more than a shiny new bridge," said Allison. "I know they've sold plenty of lots but there are still only a handful of houses. It's like a ghost town over there. By the way, when can we go over to dinner with my new friend? It would be a change of pace and you'd get an inside look at the place, so to speak."

"Maybe tomorrow. I'll have to see. So what else did you do today?"

"Oh I walked around town, organized my notes and started my article. I'm calling it The Hidden Side of Florida. So that was my day... Oh, and a man tried to pick me up."

"What?"

"He asked me to go to a speakeasy with him."

"What?"

"You said that already."

"Well, it bears repeating. Where did he get off trying to..."

"Now, Max. Put the white horse back in the stable. I don't need rescuing. I'm sure Julian is harmless."

"Oh, so you're calling him Julian now?"

"Well it *is* his name. Besides, he knows all about Florida, or so he says."

"I don't believe this. I'm running around Florida all day. I couldn't find Bubba and I still haven't found the Invisible Man, but you find an admirer while sitting in a hotel lobby."

"It's a gift."

"All right, all right. I suppose you know what you're doing. So assuming you had enough time, what with fending off admirers all day, did you make progress on the article? Do you have enough material?"

"Max, my problem isn't going to be finding things to put in the article, my problem is going to be deciding what to leave out!"

"Ah. An embarrassment of riches, eh?"

"You said it. I've got real estate tycoons selling lots, con men selling underwater property, bootleggers supplying the speakeasies, tin can tourists living in tents and travel caravans, crackers herding cattle in the swamps, and the well to do living it up in fancy Flagler hotels. Whew!"

"Not to mention a serial killer actively thinning the herd."

"Oh, yes; the Invisible Man. Any progress there?"

Max told her about Carl the canoe seller and the resulting narrowing of the suspect list to four.

"I also made a telephone call to Doris the secretary to Mr. Daniels, the man killed in the elevator. She already told me there was a call from a previously unknown man to Daniels a few days before the murder. I asked her to go through his personal notes and any appointment book he might have kept."

"What is she looking for?"

"An appointment with that same man, especially if it was on the day of the murder."

"All very logical," said Allison, "but are you certain he killer is really an unhappy real estate investor?"

Max slowly shook his head and looked out over the water. "No, I'm not, but at the moment it seems like the most likely explanation."

Allison grasped his hand.

"Max, I know this is a really difficult case and I know it isn't going the way you'd like. I also know you don't want to let Glenn Curtiss down."

"Not to mention the future victims that could soon be dead if I can't come up with a suspect in short order," said Max.

"Of course, but every case looks impossible at first and you've figured it out in the end. Look at the double murder in the locked room in Moorestown a few years ago. Nothing made sense in that case until you found the answer. And how about the lighthouse keeper near Crisfield? If you hadn't untangled that little case two of your oldest pals would have been framed for it. And the Connelly murder in New York. The whole city was buzzing about it and the suspect list was longer than a moneylender's memory, but you solved it. High stakes are nothing new for you; neither are contradictory facts. Glenn Curtiss has faith in you and so do I."

"I'll bet you say that to all the frustrated investigators," Max grinned, "but I don't really have to be bucked up at this point. You did that last night. No, I'm not really having a long dark night of the soul. I'm fine. I just can't help thinking of how important this case is."

"Fair enough. I'm just doing my 'for better or for worse' duties."

"I appreciate it, but maybe we'd better get back to the hotel. I have to call Glenn and tell him about the latest developments."

"It wouldn't hurt to let D.P. Davis in on it as well. You might ask him about the angry customer I heard about at the office yesterday."

"Sure, what's another suspect, give or take?"

Much later, Max and Allison lay in bed in their room listening to the birds and the traffic outside. The ceiling fan turned slowly and a damp breeze rustled the window curtains.

"So what did Glenn Curtiss say?"

"Mmmmm," said Max.

"A bit inarticulate for an aviation pioneer, I must say."

Max laughed. "That sound wasn't Curtiss talking; that was Max savoring the moment."

"You and me both," said Allison.

"But since you asked, he was happy we're finally getting some decent leads. Of course just getting leads isn't enough. We've got to get the killer."

"All in good time my love, all in good time."

They were quiet for a few minutes. Max drew her close.

"Allison, do you ever get tired of chasing around with me on murder cases?"

"Do you ever get tired of what we just did?"

"It's hardly the same thing."

"Well I suppose that usually your murder cases take a bit longer to, shall we say, come to a conclusion."

"All right. I really don't think we need to pursue this further."

"Mmmmm."

Chapter 20
Chipping away

The next morning was cool and cloudy. Max was sitting in Atley's office looking over the reports on property buyers who had complained or threatened real estate people.

"Max, we heard back from the Orlando police. You asked them to check the hardware stores and gun shops to see if they sold a pistol silencer in the two weeks before the elevator murder."

"And?"

"They reported a sale of a Maxim silencer at Leo's Hardware on Chase Street. A man pretty much matching the description of the guy who bought the canoe paid $3.95 cash. Said he was shooting rats in his backyard pigeon coop and didn't want to disturb the neighbors."

"Sounds like a model citizen," Max remarked. "Oh; I meant to tell you, I placed a call to Doris in Orlando after you left yesterday. I asked her to go through Mr. Daniels's notes and papers on his desk and see if there is any mention of this Morrison who shows up in the telephone log before the elevator murder."

"You think he's our man?"

"He might be. We'll have to see. If I'm right, I'll be able to tell you how the Invisible Man committed the elevator murder. She should have something this morning. We'll just have to wait."

"Yeah, we still have two other murders to solve. Speaking of which, that was a good bit of detective work with that canoe, Max" said Atley. "But assuming you're right and the canoe was used in the murder, I still don't see how the killer paddled out to the middle of the lake, killed Godfrey, then paddled back without anyone seeing him. When I asked you before, you said he did it by geometry. What in the hell does that mean?"

"It's very simple," said Max, still thumbing through the reports. "Godfrey was sitting in his boat about a half mile away from the marina. If you drew a line between the marina and the boat and extended that line, it would hit the shoreline just about where the canoe was launched. In other words, because of the distance and the positions, Godfrey and his boat actually screened the canoe from being seen from the marina."

"And the killer planned it that way?"

"Yes. To get that canoe where we found it required a longish drag through the woods. He could have launched it in several places that were much closer to the access road, but he needed to be hidden from the marina. Remember Ed the marina owner told us about the stranger who asked about the point? I believe the Invisible Man scouted the place and decided exactly where to launch that canoe so it wouldn't be seen from the marina."

"But how could he kill Godfrey without being seen?"

"It was a blunt instrument, maybe even the canoe paddle. All he had to do was to paddle out, pretend he needed help, then club Godfrey when his back was turned. Remember, it was a week day and the lake was empty. As for Ed at the marina, he could see the canoe, but at that distance, the killer was indistinguishable from his victim. Then the Invisible Man paddled back and stashed the canoe where we found it."

Atley sighed. "So as of right now we have three murders, a vague description of our man and a strong indication he comes from Virginia and is one of four suspects. We..."

"Wait a minute," said Max. "Something just occurred to me. Which of our victims did the suspects deal with? I don't see it in here."

"Does it matter?"

"It might matter a lot," said Max. "See, someone out for revenge, if that's the motive, would probably go after the object of his anger first. I think the first murder was the most important to the killer and it was the sloppiest. I doubt that the victim having a gun was part of the plan, otherwise, why use a knife, and I'll bet the locked room was a happy accident as far as the killer is concerned. I'm starting to think the whole impossible crime series was almost an afterthought when he saw the sensation the first crime caused and realized he could start a reign of terror against the whole industry."

"That's one hell of a theory, Max."

"That's the way it looks. But what about which suspect dealt with which real estate seller? Do we have that information?"

"Let me look at the files." Atley picked up the files and started rustling the papers.

"Yeah, here it is, down the bottom. It looks like. Sean McGuiness bought his property through Godfrey, the one killed at the lake; Ryan Summers bought his property from Russo, the first victim, Mario Carpellini bought his through Daniels, the elevator victim, and Ronald Anderson...say, that's interesting."

"What?"

"I didn't notice it before, but Ronald Anderson owns three properties and he bought them from three different real estate people and guess who they were."

"Surprise me."

"Russo, Godfrey, and Daniels, the three victims."

Chapter 21
A night at the Zorayda

"Max, I'm so excited. I haven't been to a speakeasy in ages, let alone one that looks like a Moorish palace."

In their room that night, Max and Allison prepared to go to the Zorayda Club, partly for the experience, and partly because Atley had assured Max there was often good information to be had.

"Well, it may not be up to the standards of Bemis's General Store and Betty Bemis's sandwiches in St Michaels," said Max, "but I've heard good things about it."

Allison pulled on a pair of white elbow length gloves and stood in front of a mirror. Her slinky silver dress, combined with her movie star good looks were too much for Max.

"You know, they have great room service here. We could stay in and...."

She leaned over and kissed him on the cheek. "All in good time, my love. All in good time. First the fun, and then... even more fun. As Mr. Jolson so eloquently put it, 'You ain't seen nothin' yet!'."

"Pleasure before pleasure, I suppose. Are you ready, or are there still levels of perfection you have not yet attained?"

She looked in the mirror one last time and straightened a strand of hair that didn't really need it.

"Lead on, Macduff."

"Isn't the line 'Lay on Macduff.'?"

"It is, but I didn't want to give you any ideas."

127

The Zorayda Club was only a block away, so they walked through the cool night air.

"Max, isn't St Augustine a beautiful place? All this Moorish architecture and fountains."

"Yes, Henry Flagler and his railroad certainly did the place proud, and D.P. Davis is doing his part as well."

"Oh, Max. I almost forgot. We have to go to dinner at Davis Shores."

"All right. Maybe tomorrow night. Well, this has to be it."

They stopped in front of a two story masonry building with pointed arch windows, Moorish balconies, and a pointed arch gate where a front door would usually be.

"As advertised," said Max. "Well, let's see if they let a couple of infidels come in."

They stepped into a small ante chamber and were greeted by a huge doorman dressed in an Arabian Knights costume complete with a nasty-looking scimitar.

"Welcome to the Zorayda Club," he said in a rumbling voice. "May you and your camels find rest and entertainment within."

"Our camels sniff the evening and are glad. Open the gates O watchman of the night," said Allison, as Max ushered her inside.

"Remember to send a thank you note to your literature professor at Goucher," Max mumbled.

"I must say, they certainly get into the spirit of...oh, my!" Allison was momentarily rendered speechless by the sight in front of them.

The Zorayda Club was built around a large interior courtyard/atrium, two stories high and built with an arched gallery all around the upper level, At the center of the atrium was a small tiled pool in the shape of an eight pointed star, and in the center of the pool was a fountain splashing merrily. Café tables, sofas and cushions were placed around the space and occupied by elegantly dressed couples chatting and drinking from what appeared to be jeweled cups. A bar could be seen in a room off the courtyard and several craps tables were doing a lively business in another. Brightly lit slot machines were placed in clusters anywhere there was extra space, their bells and clattering coins competing with the shouts from the craps tables.

"Maybe the doorman was really a genie," said Allison. "This place is like another world. I don't know what the food and drink is like, but the atmosphere is the eel's eyebrows."

Just then, a jazz band somewhere out of sight started up in yet another room off of the courtyard, adding yet another layer of noise and excitement.

"Maybe we should find a table," said Max above the music.

"Lead on, O Master of the Caravan."

"I don't see any camels," Max remarked. "I guess the racket scared them away."

They found a table near the fountain and gave their order to a waiter who looked like Ali Baba. The food and drinks soon appeared and the evening was on its way.

"We should open a place like this in St Michaels," said Allison. "It would be just the thing for a night out after a hard day oystering."

"I think we've got enough local color," said Max.

"I suppose we won't be doing much of this with a baby," said Allison, uncertainly.

Max shrugged. "Babies aren't big on going to speakeasies as far as I know, but I think there will be other compensations. That is, assuming..."

"Assuming what?"

"Nothing. Never mind."

"You're worried about it aren't you Max?"

"No; of course not, I just..."

"I am too. What if we're terrible parents? What if...if we can't even have children?"

"Well, at least both of those things can't be true. Look, everyone gets cold feet about this sort of thing from time to time. We'll be fine."

She smiled. "Of course you're right. And the night is young."

Max looked around. "If you could excuse me a minute, I need to talk to the bartender before the band starts up again. Atley says he has some prime gossip that might help the case. I'll be right back."

The bartender turned out to be practically the only staff member not dressed as if he just stepped off of a magic carpet. He was a stocky man with a beard stubble and an accent that seemed to be from New England, obviously a transplant from the north.

"So I understand from the sheriff that you have some information about the Invisible Man." Max had decided on the direct approach.

The bartender looked at him. "Maybe, if I can remember."

Max took his cue and produced a fiver.

The bartender motioned to the assistant to take over for him temporarily, and leaned over the bar towards Max.

"I didn't think anything of it at the time, because it was about a week before that guy got killed in his locked office up in Jax."

"Jacksonville?"

"Right. Anyway, this guy is in here and it's wicked raining outside, so it's a slow night. He has a couple of drinks, then starts talking, almost to himself. Says what a crime it is that so many people got conned into investing in real estate that proves worthless. I just nodded in sympathy. I mean, I get more good tips from listening to sob stories than I ever get from serving up drinks."

Now it was Max's turn to nod sympathetically.

"He started talking about how someone could work his whole life and lose everything in one bad investment. Said it was a damned crime. Then he smiled a little and said that the time was coming that the people selling phony real estate would get what was coming to them; that they wouldn't be able to cheat anyone else. Of course, there's nothing like a few drinks to get people to say dumb things. They're going to do this or they're going to do that. Like I said, I thought it was just belly aching until that guy got murdered a week later. That kind of gave me the creeps. Anyway, I haven't seen the guy since."

"Did this guy have a name?" Max asked.

"Never said."

"What did he look like?"

"Brown hair; average height and build; clean shaven...nothing special. Oh, wait a minute. He had a gold ring on his right hand and the ring had this anchor on it."

"Anchor?"

"Yeah. It was sort of at an angle. Like maybe he was in the Navy or something. I noticed because I was looking at his glass to see if he needed a refill and his hand was on it."

Out in the courtyard, Allison was sipping her drink and enjoying the atmosphere when she heard a familiar voice."

"Allison! Why this is wonderful."

She turned and saw Julian DeKuyper standing by her side, still wearing a white suit.

"Oh, hello, Julian. I told you my husband was taking me here."

Julian slid into a chair at the table. "Isn't this a wonderful place? It makes you think you're in Seville or some place like that, doesn't it?"

"It has pizazz. No doubt about that."

"It has a lot more now that you're here. So tell me Allison, how are you finding St Augustine?"

"Oh, I just walk out of the hotel and there it is. You can't miss it."

"Ha ha. How delightful," said Julian, smiling broader than ever. "You are witty as well as beautiful. May I buy you a drink?"

"I have one already."

"Ah. So you do. Well, Allison, I think you will find that St Augustine is a fascinating place, just the sort of place someone from up north would want as a second home, or even a first one."

"Yes. I've been to Davis Shores. Very impressive."

"Oh, yes a splendid place, no doubt, but I have a feeling your standards are very high. You would be happier with a waterfront estate; a place where someone as lovely as you would..."

"Julian, have I not made it clear that I'm a married woman? The reference to my husband should have tipped you off."

"So much the better! You and your husband can share the Florida dream. Just look at the sort of properties that are available."

132

With that, Julian DeKuyper produced brochures and photographs of various local properties and spread them on the table. Allison burst out laughing.

"So this is what all the gallant gentleman act was about? You want to sell me property?"

"Dear lady, I told you my intentions were honorable."

"I'm glad to hear that," said Max, who had just appeared behind Allison.

"Ah, Mr. Hurlcck. I was just showing your charming wife some of the wonderful properties still available in this most delightful area."

"So you sell real estate?"

"Only the best real estate. Julian DeKuyper at your service, Mr. Hurlock."

"Max," said Alliscn, "Julian here is a regular at the Zorayda."

Max sat next to Allison. "Really? Have you seen a man about my size and wearing a gold ring with an anchor on it? I believe this man was in the market for some property at one time."

"I deal in high end properties, Mr. Hurlock. Many of my clients wear gold rings, but I don't recall one with an anchor on it. Is this man a friend of yours?"

"Hardly. I'd just like to find him. Tell me. Have any of your clients been dissatisfied?"

"I strive to give satisfaction, Mr. Hurlock, after all..."

"What I mean is if any of the people to whom you've sold are having trouble making the payments."

"Oh, one or two have had some reversals, but such things are inevitable.'

"Have any of them threatened you?"

"You're talking abcut the Invisible Man aren't you? That nut running around killing real estate people?

Well, no. No one I deal with has ever been *that* unhappy."

"Does the situation surprise you?"

"The intensity does, of course, but I'm not really surprised someone is lashing out at others for his own bad decision. No one complained as long as the prices kept going up, but now that they've stalled, suddenly the real estate people are villains. I imagine a stockbroker has the same problem. Say, what is your interest? Are you with the police?"

"I'm just a private citizen taking an interest in local affairs," said Max.

Julian smiled at him slyly, and rose to leave. "Of course," he said, in a tone that suggested that his next words might be "and I'm the King of Romania."

"Mr. DeKuyper" said Max, handing him a card, "I'd be obliged if you'd let me know if you remember or hear of the man with the anchor on his ring."

Julian bowed slightly. "Certainly. Good night Mr. Hurlock...Allison."

Max shook his head as he watched Julian DeKuyper disappear across the smoky room.

"If I could find the killer half as fast as you find admirers, we'd be home by now."

Allison grasped his arm. "You're sexy when you're jealous."

"No; I'm jealous when you're sexy."

"So what's this about a ring with an anchor?"

"The bartender had a patron threatening retribution upon all real estate people in Florida just before the murder started. The man was wearing a gold ring with an anchor."

"Interesting," said Allison.

"Yes; especially since one of our suspects is in the Navy."

Chapter 22
Death in the air

The next morning was muggy as the rising sun pushed through a haze. Max and Allison got some coffee and some pastries and had breakfast in the Plaza de la Constitution, a park area across the street from the   Alcazar. The Plaza featured shade trees, some old cannons, and a few monuments among the greenery. Nearby a newspaper boy was shouting about his wares.

"Read all about it. Governor demands action on Invisible Man murders. Will appoint task force!"

"What? Paper here!"

Max gave the boy a nickel, took a newspaper and scanned the article.

"The governor must be getting a lot of pressure. He's setting up some sort of task force to take over the investigation."

"That doesn't sound good," said Allison.

Max folded up the newspaper. "On the contrary. It s*ounds* very good, and will give the public the impression of a dynamic governor taking decisive action. I just don't think it will work that well in practice."

"Too many cooks spoiling the broth?" said Allison.

"Exactly; and too much information being made public. The more people involved, the more likely it will be that at least one of them will blab too much to the press. The killer will be able to follow the investigation in the news and plan accordingly."

"You'll just have to catch the killer before the task force can mess things up too badly."

"Yes," said Max. "A little more pressure to contend with; just what we needed. I think I'd better get over to Atley's office and see if anything new came in overnight. What about you?"

"I'll stick around here and try to get my article organized. Then I'll know where I need to go to fill in the blanks."

"Good plan," said Max. "We both have quite a few blanks to fill in."

In a wooded area thirty miles south of Lake George meanwhile, the wind hissed softly through the canopy of tree branches overhead, and angled shafts of early-morning sunlight speckled the forest floor in a scene that looked like some majestic green cathedral. All that was needed was a choir. In this tranquil scene, some moss covered twigs cracked softly underfoot as two men slowly pushed their way through the underbrush carrying rifles.

"So you gonna get a deer today, or what?" said one of the men.

The second man smiled and shifted his deer rifle to his other hand. "You just watch and see how it's done. Them deer better hide."

"Shoot. The only way you gonna get a deer is if the damned thing dies of old age in front of you. Either that or he'll die laughin' when you miss him."

"Bushwa. I know I got skunked the last time, but this is another day. You can't keep a good man down."

"Yeah. Maybe you'll get lucky and meet a whitetail with no instinct for self-preservation. See any tracks yet?"

"Naw. Just a lot of leaves and sticks and pine needles, but there are plenty of deer around this area. You just keep your eyes peeled."

"There's a little clearing up ahead by the stream. That should be a good place. They come there to drink."

"I could use a drink myself."

They pushed aside the last branches and were in the clearing.

"Let's rest a spell and keep our eyes open in case one of 'em might be stopping by for a drink."

"Sure, if you're tired already."

"Damn it, I ain't tired. I just think we should look and listen a while."

"All right Daniel Boone. Maybe we can smell 'em."

"More likely they'll smell us first. I'll bet you ain't washed that shirt since the last time."

"Of course not. This here's my lucky shirt."

They sat with their backs against a large tree and savored the quiet. In the distance, a bird sang, but otherwise, all was still except the rustling of the trees.

"Sure is quiet. Guess that means nobody else is getting deer either."

"I heard a few shots earlier. Hope it wasn't somebody else baggin' our deer."

"Well, if it was, it's somebody else's deer now, I guess."

The second hunter put his hands behind his head and slipped a little lower.

"Yeah, not a bad way to spend the day. Beats cuttin' the grass. Way I figure it, a man has to get out in the woods every now and again to breathe the air and recharge his batteries, so to speak. If you happen to get a deer, why that's a bonus."

"Yeah, I guess. Of course,..." He stopped abruptly, squinting above him.

"What's the matter?"

"Look up into the branches of this tree. Do you see that stickin' out of the leaves?"

"Yeah, I do see something. What is that? Looks like...a shoe. A shoe up in a danged tree?"

In a second, they scrambled to their feet and moved away from the base of the tree for a better look."

"Damn. That's not just a shoe; that's some guy up in the tree, and I think he's dead! Look how he's slumped over that branch."

"How in the hell did he get up there? That must be close to 20 feet above the ground. Do you think he fell out of an airplane?"

"I dunno, but we better get the cops here before somebody blames us."

They hurried out of the clearing, fighting the urge to look back over their shoulders.

Atley was reading a message as Max arrived.

"Good news, Max. I found a telegram from Norfolk when I arrived a little while ago. It came in last night. Our suspect list is now down to three. The Coast Guard arrested Sean McGuiness yesterday."

"Isn't he the suspected bootlegger?" Max asked.

"That's the one. He was on a ship from Cuba bringing in a load of illegal rum. It seems that while the ship was waiting for the rumrunners to come and unload, the navigator got into the cargo and started nipping at it. He got spifflicated enough to affect his navigation and didn't realize that the ship had wandered into U.S. territorial waters. The Coast Guard didn't make that mistake; they boarded the vessel and impounded the cargo. McGuiness was on board, and since the ship had been underway since leaving Havana a week ago, McGuiness is in the clear."

"At least as far as the murders are concerned," said Max. "Violations of the Prohibition law are another matter. Well, I found out something at the Zoraya last night that might be of interest."

Max told Atley about the bartenders tale of the man with the gold ring and the anchor.

"An anchor you say? That would seem to point to Mario Carpellini, the missing Navy man."

"It might," said Max. "Say, did you hear about the Governor's Task Force?"

"Yeah, I got a call just before you got here. He's going to announce the members this afternoon."

"Are we going to be on it?" Max asked.

"The Governors a politician, but he's no fool. He knows a task force would be like expecting a committee to solve the case, but he wants to do something. He's going to pretty much leave us alone to do things our way, but make me a member of the task force so he can take credit when the case is solved."

"So who else is involved?"

"Mostly local sheriffs and police chiefs is the word I got. I'll know more this afternoon. You'll probably be a member, at least informally, so the Governor can say he's gathering experts from all over to combat the problem. If we're lucky, it'll just be a formal version of what we're already doing."

"I don't like that idea," said Max. "I'd rather work without a lot of attention. I have more freedom that way."

"You and me both."

"Sheriff, there's a call for you from Marion. They say it's urgent."

"All right. Sheriff Atley here. Yes...when...where? Wait a minute, where did you say it was? Holy... We'll be there in an hour."

He hung up the phone and turned to Max.

"Looks like the Task Force just got themselves another task. The Invisible Man has gotten another one. A couple of deer hunters found a body in the woods in the Ocala National Forest near Marion; looks like he was shot."

"What makes you think it was the work of the Invisible Man and not just a hunting accident?" Max asked.

"The victim was Henry LaPointe, president of LaPointe Properties. And there is one more thing."

"And what is that?"

"The body was draped over a tree limb 15 feet in the air."

Max nodded. "That sounds like our boy, all right. Well, we'd better get down there before the press and the medical examiner mess up the evidence."

On the way to the car, Atley threw up his arms in frustration. "What in the blue blazes is going on? The body was way up in a tree and there was no ladder or rope or anything that might account for how it got there. I'm telling you, Max, I'm starting to think this guy really is invisible, and a damned magician besides. I mean, first he stabs a man who is shooting at him in a small locked room, then somehow gets out unharmed with the door still locked from the inside, then he kills another victim in the middle of a lake in broad daylight without being seen..."

"We know how he did that," Max reminded him.

But Atley was off and running. "...then he kills another man in a danged elevator between floors, and now he somehow shoots a man and hangs his body up in a tree. It's almost supernatural."

"No it isn't," said Max. "It's all planned. Every murder has a logical explanation. They seem impossible, because that's what the killer wants, but once you figure out how it was done, you'll slap yourself in the forehead because it was so obvious."

"That's all well and good, just so long's the governor doesn't slap me first."

Allison sat in the lobby of the hotel going through her notes.

"Now what is the angle for this article?" she mumbled to herself. "The Hidden Side of Florida, The Pot of Gold at the End of the Rainbow? Maybe the Florida the tourists never see? Or how about Clouds over the Sunshine State? Hmmm...not bad." Allison made some notes on her pad in her lap. As she stared at the note she had made, she started thinking once again, of the prospect of starting a family with Max, musing on the fact that parenthood was an important job that required absolutely no training. She had to admit, it was a little scary.

"I wonder if I'll be any good at it?"

"What are you doing?" came a squeaky voice.

Allison looked up to see a small head peeking at her over the back of a nearby couch. The head belonged to a boy about four years old and was wearing a red cowboy hat.

"Oh, hello," said Allison. "What's your name?"

"Billy. My Mommy and Daddy are taking me to the beach."

Allison nodded "I see. Are you going to round up some cattle when you get there?"

"Cattle?"

"Never mind. I suppose that's your mother and father over at the desk checking in?"

"I hurt my knee. What are you drawing? Can you make a picture of a cowboy?"

"I don't know. I've never tried."

"I like cowboys. They get to ride on horses!"

"I met a cowboy yesterday," said Allison. "He has a ranch near here."

The boy's eyed widened. "Did he have a horse?"

"I suppose he did, but he left it home."

The boy looked disappointed, but recovered quickly. "Do you have any boys or girls?"

Allison could feel her face redden slightly. "Well, no; no yet, but I'm planning on having one or two."

"How are you going to get them?"

"Oh, the usual way, I guess."

"How?"

"Can we talk about something else?"

"Look; I can stand on my head." Billy demonstrated before falling over and almost knocking over a lamp.

"My daddy has really big feet," he announced when he was back on the sofa again.

"Billy, maybe you shouldn't tell people that. Look, I'll try to draw you a cowboy on my pad."

"Don't forget the horse."

Billy watched her effort intensely, then scrunched up his nose. "What's the matter with him? Is he sick?"

"I told you I never drew a cowboy before."

"Billy! Stop bothering that lady," came a voice. Billy's mother had appeared, looking somewhat exasperated.

"I'm sorry. Billy likes to talk and he can be something of a pest at times," the mother explained, taking Billy by the hand.

"Oh, that's all right," said Allison. "He was helping me develop my drawing skills. Good bye, Billy. Nice talking to you."

As Billy was led away, Allison heard him tell his mother, "Mommy, that lady said I shouldn't tell people about daddy's big feet."

Allison sighed. She felt wrung out by her mercifully brief encounter with Billy. Maybe there was more to this parenting thing than she thought.

Max looked around the woods as he and Atley followed Billings, the local constable to the crime scene. Twigs cracked and leaves rustled under their feet.

"It's just up ahead a little ways. The press doesn't know about this yet, but once they do, they'll be all over it. The medical examiner took the body away, but I had them take a lot of photographs first, just like you said." Billings assured them. "The victim was shot once and was draped over a limb."

"How was he oriented?" Max asked.

"Well, he was lying so that his stomach was in contact with the tree branch. His head and arms were hanging over one side and his legs and feet on the other."

"Have you notified his wife?" Atley asked.

"Yes, I did, and I got some questions in once she settled down. She said he was out there hunting deer himself. He used to go out every day during deer season. He was dressed in hunting clothes when we found him, but we never found his gun, so we know we didn't shoot himself accidentally."

"I think we're here," said Max. "I see a couple of police standing by that tree up ahead, and a ladder against the trunk."

"That's right," said Billings. "That's the tree, and that's the limb the body was draped over, the one on the left about 16 feet above the ground."

"You measured?" Max asked.

"Twice."

"And I assume that ladder wasn't here when the body was found?"

"No," said Billings. "We brought the ladder to get the body down and to be able to investigate. We used a block and tackle tied to the limb above."

"So Mr. LaPointe went out hunting and wound up shot to death up in a tree without his rifle. Did you turn up any way that Mr. LaPointe could have gotten into that tree?" Atley asked.

Billings shook his head glumly. "No, nothing. There was no ladder, no rope, nothing at all. It's as if he just flew up there."

Max started walking around the tree looking at the limb, then the bark and the ground. Several times he squatted and seemed to be examining the dirt.

"Could he have climbed up on his own and then been shot, and then slumped over the branch?" Atley continued.

"I...I guess so," said Billings uncertainly.

Max returned and Atley told him his theory that LaPointe had climbed on his own, been shot, then slumped over the branch. Max shook his head.

"No," said Max. "That's not what happened. He was placed over that branch. Look up at the location of the branch in relation to the ones around it. There isn't another branch closer than maybe five feet away. There is no branch he could have been stranding on that is close enough to allow him to collapse over that branch the way he was found. Even if he had been standing or sitting on the branch where he was found, he would never have slumped over the branch with his head and body on one side and his legs on the other; he would have fallen off completely, or wound up straddling and lying parallel to the branch."

Atley scratched his head. "Well, I guess..."

"Constable Billings," said Max, "can you get several men to conduct a search?"

Billings nodded. I guess I can find a few. "Er...search where ar_d for what?"

"Search outward from the tree, concentrating in that direction." Max pointed eastwards.

"What are we looking for, Mr. Hurlock?"

"A lightweight ladder."

"Max, what in the world...?"

"Come look over here at the base of the tree," said Max. They walked over and looked at the base of the tree in a puzzled manner.

"Now look at the ladder. See how the legs sink a little into the soft gro_nd?" said Max, pointing.

"Max, the police brought that ladder They said so."

"Now look about a foot to the right. There are two more holes just about far enough apart to be from a ladder."

"So? Maybe the locals put the ladder there first, then moved it."

"Look closer. These holes are smaller than the legs of the ladder the police brought. They were left by another ladder, a ladder that was removed and probably taken in tha_ direction."

"Tarnation, Max; how can you tell which way they took the ladder?"

"If you look at the holes, you can see they are wider on one side because whatever was in them was pulled in that direction as it was removed. That's probably because they were taking the ladder in that same direction."

"So if we find that ladder it will show that the killer carried the body up into the tree?"

"I doubt it," said Max. "Billings told me LaPointe was a hefty man. He'd be hard to carry vertically. Besides, if two men had been on the ladder at once, the holes in the ground would have been much deeper. No, Mr. LaPointe climbed up there himself. Then he was shot and draped over the tree branch."

"What? How in the world did the killer arrange that?"

"I have an idea, but let's see what the search turns up."

Atley shook his head. "Well, if Mario Carpellini really is the Invisible Man, he hasn't lost his touch."

"No," said Max, "and I'm afraid the only way he'll lose his touch if for us to stop him. While we wait for the search, let me show you a couple of more things around the tree. See those scratches about a foot or so below the branch? Keep them in mind. I think they're the key to the Invisible Man's latest impossible crime."

They walked around the area for another ten minutes or so, but found nothing of interest.

"You can't really track footprints in this forest litter on the ground unless you're Daniel Boone maybe," said Atley. "Let's hope you're right about which way they took that other ladder."

"Looks like a couple of the searchers have returned, and look what they have with them."

"A ladder," said Atley, "just like you said."

Billings spoke with the men briefly, then to Max and Atley.

"The boys found this in some bushes maybe a half mile away. Haven't tried to see if the legs fit the holes you found under the tree, but I have a feelin' they will."

Max nodded. "It looks that way. Did they find anything else?"

"No, but I have a couple of other men still looking."

"All right," said Max, "but I think there's one more object out there waiting to be found. Wait a minute. Someone else is coming back and look what he's carrying."

"I know what that is," said Atley. "I know exactly what it is. That Carpellini is one clever boy."

"Exactly," said Max. "You see..."

Atley swung his head around. "Who the hell is that now?"

Three men suddenly appeared noisily pushing through the undergrowth. The press had gotten wind of the latest murder. And were wasting no time

"Where's the body?"

"Have you found any clues?"

"Do you have any leads?"

"You there, are you the sheriff?" said one of the men to Atley.

"Yes, sir," Atley answered.

"Is this the work of the Invisible Man?"

"We are still investigating,"

"What was the victim's name?"

"I'm afraid that's withheld pending notification of next of kin."

"How do you spell your name?"

"A-T-L-E-Y."

"Do you have any suspects?"

"That is under investigation as well."

"I understand the victim was found up in a tree. How did he get there?"

"We are still investigating. Come on fellas. I have to get back to work."

While this was going on, one of the other reporters noticed Max looking around by the tree trunk and approached him, pad in hand.

"Say, are you somebody?"

Max just smiled. "Don't see a badge, do you? I'm just a curious citizen."

The reporter put his notebook away and lit a cigarette. "Well, the sheriff over there isn't much better. All he says is they're investigating. Seems to me we need less investigating and more discovering. This Invisible Man is making monkeys out the sheriff and all the others trying to find him."

"So far," said Max.

"What do you mean, so far?" said the reporter. "You have to admit that this killer is smarter than the police."

Max shook his head slowly and turned to walk away. "The jails are full of people who thought they were smarter than the police. And you can quote that."

Chapter 23
The frenzy

When they got back to the Sheriff's office, a telegram was waiting for Atley summoning him to Tallahassee to serve as part of the backdrop for the governor's announcement the next morning.

"Looks like I'm formally on the Task Force, Max, but this part is interesting. He requests that you be a 'consultant' to the Task Force. Pretty slick. That way he gets to continue to have your help without opening himself up to criticism for packing the Task Force with out-of-state private eyes. The PIs down here would holler."

"This is why I stay away from politics," said Max. "Besides, I'm not a private detective; I'm an investigator. So what will change?"

Atley put the message down on the desk. "Nothing really. I'll just have more people to report to. I worked with Governor Martin on a couple of things when he was the mayor of Jacksonville, so he wants to leave me informally in charge. I just have to stand there with the others at Tallahassee tomorrow and then get back here."

"All right. Meanwhile, I'd like to look at the crime scene photos and the files on the suspects again."

"Sure thing, Max. I'll get them and you can go over them in the interview room."

Max had only been in the room with the files for about ten minutes when Atley appeared in the doorway.

"Max, our job just got easier. I got a call from the police in Portland, Oregon. They found Ryan Summers."

"In Oregon? Where was he all this time?"

"He took his wife there about two months ago to make a new start. He was living under an alias to throw creditors off the scent. That's why it took so long to find him."

"So does he have an alibi for the murders?" Max asked.

"That *is* his alibi. He was living in Oregon. The police talked to a bunch of his neighbors and they all confirm that he appeared there about the time he says and was never gone for more than a day or so. He couldn't be the killer, so we can cross him off the list."

"And then there were two," said Max, "Mario Carpellini and Ronald Anderson. The Task Force will start with the field considerably narrowed down."

Max called Glenn Curtiss to tell him about the latest developments. Curtiss was gloomy. "This guy is clever, Max. I have a feeling that the only way to catch him is to catch him in the act somehow. It's like some of the engines I've worked on. If they had a problem you could see and hear, you could usually fix it, but sometimes the things would only act up when the airplane was in the sky and purr like a kitten on the ground. That's why I say you have to catch him in the act, but I have no idea how to do that."

"I planted an anonymous quote with a reporter today. If he uses it, it may help to goad the Invisible Man into carelessness," said Max. "Overconfidence is usually what does in these kind of killers."

"It can't hurt. I'm sure the killer is reading the papers faithfully, if only to see his exploits in print. Any other irons in the fire, Max?"

"I'm trying to figure out who the next victim might be, but there are so many possibilities. If only I could figure out his selection process, I might have a chance to stop him."

"Well, the Task Force might be just the thing. John Martin has given you a gift. The high profile people on the Task Force will draw the press away from you and Atley. Who knows? They might even turn up something you can use. Good luck, Max. Keep your nose up and your tail down."

Max then called D.P. Davis's office and set up a meeting for lunch the next day to keep him up to date and to ask about the disgruntled buyer Allison had heard about.

That night, Max took Allison to a small place in the old Spanish city. The rickety tables each had a candle and innumerable scars and scratches from meals past. They ordered the Jambalaya, which had become a favorite with both of them and Allison looked thoughtful as they waited for the food.

"Anything wrong?" Max asked. "You seem like something's bothering you."

She smiled in a distracted way. "I suppose I'm having that long dark night of the soul I thought you were having before."

"Don't tell me you're worrying about the baby project?"

"Well, it is uncharted territory for us. I'm not sure we're prepared for an addition."

"So whoever is? You do your best and learn as you go along. Somehow the children survive in spite of their parents."

"I guess so, but there was this little boy in the lobby today. He came up to me and started talking. It was so awkward; I just didn't know what to say to him. It was like talking to a Martian or something. I got all tongue tied. What kind of a mother can't talk to a child?"

"Looks like we both have sort of cold feet, but we've never let that stop us. We didn't know how to do a lot of things like flying, heating an old house in the winter, traveling on steamships, or dealing with some of the local characters in St Michaels and Easton, but we learned because we did it together, and because we picked ourselves up and dusted ourselves off when we did it wrong the first time. We'll do this, too."

She took his hand and smiled. "I'm seeing the doctor as soon as we get back. If it's good news, I'll bake you a cake."

"Chocolate icing?"

"You got it."

Later, as they walked back to the Alcazar, the conversation came back to the murders.

"So that's how it stands," said Max. "We have the suspects narrowed down to two, but we can't seem to find either one of them. If I could only figure out where he's getting his information, maybe I could figure out where he plans to strike next."

"I thought he was observing his victims and gathering information that way?" said Allison.

"That's true, but where does he get his list of prospects? He might be familiar with one or two, but he's working from a list. Where did he get the list? These people he's after are not exactly celebrities. Most people, especially people living in another state have never heard of who's who in real estate, but somehow, he knows."

"Maybe the newspapers?"

"I doubt it. They might mention a developer or two in a story, but they never give any detailed information. No, there's some other source."

"A magazine article? They have lots of detail in feature articles. I ought to know; I write enough of them."

Max stopped in his tracks. "A magazine article! Of course. That would explain it. That would be all he would need."

"Of course. Someone else did the research for him. All he'd have to do would be to observe each victim and plan each crime."

"That must be what happened," said Max. "You know, if we only knew what article he was using and had a copy, we'd have a pretty good list of his victims, including the ones he hasn't gotten to yet. You're the magazine expert, Allison. Is it possible to find out?"

Allison thought for a moment. "There's an awful lot of magazines and magazine articles to sift through. Wait a minute. What about The Readers' Guide to Periodical Literature?"

"The what?"

"It's a sort of index that lists magazine articles by subject. Then you can find out where that particular article appeared and maybe look it up. They usually have them at any good library."

"Where would that be around here? Isis Dalrymple the ever knowledgeable St Michaels librarian is a long ways away."

"Her spirit is here. Before we left I asked her for the location of any local libraries in case I needed them for reference. She said to go to the Carnegie Library in Jacksonville."

"Great. I'll head up there first thing tomorrow while Atley goes to Tallahassee to have his picture taken with the governor. How about coming along with me? You know more about the world of magazines than I do."

"It's a date. Well, it's been a long day," said Allison, stretching dramatically. "I can't wait to get to bed."

Max smiled. "You are just *full* of good ideas tonight."

To describe the Governor's press conference the next morning as pandemonium would be to understate the level of confusion, outrage, accusations and just plain noise it produced.

With the number of impossible murders now up to four, and no end in sight, both the press and the public demanded answers and mostly demanded action. The fact that many had friends or relatives connected with real estate in one way or another lent an air of desperation to the event. After all, who knew where the Invisible Man would strike next?

Governor Martin, standing in front of a dozen assorted lawmen formally announced the formation of the Florida Public Safety Task Force as flashbulbs popped in his face.

Then the questions started.

"Governor, have you considered calling out the National Guard?"

"Have you assigned a guard to real estate people?"

"Has there been any communication from the killer?"

"Are there any suspects as yet?"

"When do you expect to make an arrest?"

"Why didn't you do this earlier?"

"Governor, couldn't you have done more to prevent these killings?"

The governor responded as best he could, but it was evident to everyone in the State House that day, that there were very few answers. Atley stood with the others looking stony faced, silently counting the minutes until he could get out of there.

He almost felt sorry for the governor.

There were screaming headlines in all the Florida newspapers the next day, but the Jacksonville Times probably said it best.

MARTIN ANNOUNCES TASK FORCE
KILLER STILL INVISIBLE

Max picked up a paper when he went to breakfast with Allison.

"Yikes. They're really turning up the heat on the governor," said Allison. "Let's hope you're not the one who gets burned."

"I'm still staying in the background as far as the public is concerned," said Max. "I'm just some minor out of town consultant."

"Well, you be careful. These people are getting frustrated and they're getting desperate. The longer the case goes unsolved, the more they'll be pointing fingers and looking for someone to blame Who better than an out of town meddler?"

"It won't be the first time," said Max. "It's an occupational hazard."

"Oh, that makes me feel much better," said Allison.

"Well, let's get over to the library in Jacksonville and hope we can find something that helps."

The Carnegie Library in Jacksonville was a two story limestone building with four classic Greek columns in front. Allison had called ahead and the librarian was waiting for them with a copy of The Readers' Guide to Periodical Literature. Max and Allison took it to a table in the reference section and started to search the subject index.

"All right," said Allison. "We could start with Florida, but that's too broad. We'll have hundreds of articles to sift through."

"Florida real estate would be almost as bad," said Max. "How about Florida developers?"

"Let's see...There are several articles, but they seem to be pretty general judging by the titles and the magazines they're in. Maybe Florida land sales?"

"I don't think so. You'll get a bunch of real estate advertising. How about Florida land barons?"

"A bit dramatic, but worth a try," said Allison. "No, nothing. Perhaps....wait a minute. Let's look at Florida and see what the sub headings are. Here it is."

"There's almost a whole page of subheadings," Max protested.

"But look. The Real estate sub heading has a bunch of sub headings of its own. Let's see...Real estate advertising, Real estate costs...Real estate markets...Real estate boom...That has possibilities...Real estate...Here. Look at this one."

"Real estate tycoons: The men who are transforming the face of Florida," Max read. "Bullseye."

"And look. It's in McGuffy's Magazine. They're small circulation, but fairly popular on the east coast. I submitted an article to them once. They like a lot of detail."

"What issue was this in?"

"Let me see. November 1925. Why that's just a little while before the first murder. We should look this up. I'll check with the librarian. Keep your fingers crossed that they have it on file, Max."

Allison returned shortly with the magazine in her hand. Max took it eagerly.

"Let's see. The index said it was on page 23...Here it is." Max skimmed the article in silence a moment.

"Allison I think we might have something. It has brief biographies of several Florida real estate developers, including the location of their offices, where they live, and even their hobbies."

"Who are they? Anyone you know?"

Max read through the names. "Holy cats. Listen to this; Tom Russo (the locked office) It says he often works alone at the office on weekends; Robert Godfrey (the lake) It says he likes to go fishing alone on Lake George every Thursday, Wilson Daniels (the elevator) It says he arrives every morning at the office like clockwork; Henry LaPointe (the tree) It says he looks forward to deer hunting season each year. This human interest angle gives enough information to make planning a murder easy."

Allison gasped. "Oh, Max. And that's the exact list of men murdered."

"So far," said Max "This article is a blueprint for the Invisible Man murders."

"Max, are there more names in that article?"

"Yes. Two; someone named Calvin Warfield in Melbourne. It says he has a private art gallery and he always wears a brown suit. It even has his picture..."

"And who's the other?"

"D.P. Davis."

John Reisinger

Chapter 24
D.P. Davis and the Loas

In the Mainsail Restaurant in St Augustine, D.P. Davis leaned over the table and looked at Max warily.

"So you think I'm on the list, do you?"

"You were listed in the article and the other victims were listed as well. I think the killer is using the article to compile a list of victims and to get information he can use to help plan the crimes."

Davis shook his head. "Amazing. Glenn Curtiss was right about you, Max. You are a damned good detective. That was good work. I'm really impressed."

"Mr. Davis," said Max in an exasperated voice. "I don't need you to be impressed; I need you to be alive. We have to stop this guy before he comes after you. Maybe you should hire a bodyguard until we arrest someone."

Davis waved his hand in a gesture of dismissal. "A bodyguard? Bah. At Davis Shores I wrestled a new village where people would be proud to live out of a mangrove swamp. I fought the banks, the muck, the mosquitos and the hurricanes. I didn't get where I am by running and hiding. A developer won't go far if he's afraid of his customers."

"Speaking of which, one of your managers at Davis Shores told Allison that an unhappy customer was threatening you a couple of weeks ago. What was that about?"

"Nothing much. I remember that guy. It was a sad case, but it was his problem, not mine. A man got in over his head, can't make a quick profit on a resale and can't make his payments to the bank, so he blames me. Says I shouldn't have sold him land he couldn't afford. Can you beat that? It wasn't his fault for being irresponsible; it's my fault for not restraining him. A ten year old couldn't have put it better. Anyway, he's harmless."

"I think you need to take this more seriously..."

"I told you. That palooka is harmless."

"Maybe, but somewhere out there is someone who isn't harmless."

Davis lit a cigarette. "So find him and arrest him. I'm not hiding under the bed for anybody."

After Max dropped her off back at the hotel. Allison went for a stroll around town. After having a quick lunch at a soda fountain, Allison passed by the Zorayda Club, still looking somewhat exotic, but much less mysterious in the daylight. Nearby was the Moorish elegance of the Flagler Hotel, looking like some massive wedding cake surrounded by gardens and fountains.

"Allison!"

She turned and saw Nancy, the woman she met at Davis Shores calling her. She soon caught up.

"Hey, Allison. This is wonderful. I come across to town every week or so for a change of scene. How have you been? We're still waiting for you and your husband to come by for dinner at Davis Shores."

"We will, Nancy. I promise, but Max has been so wrapped up with his business here. The fact is, he's helping the local police track down the Invisible Man killer, so you can see how his schedule might be a little erratic."

"You said it. I been following things in the newspapers. That Invisible Man's like a ghost. I don't know you catch a guy like that."

"It's been a problem," Allison was forced to admit, "but Max is chasing a few leads. He'll get to the bottom of it."

Nancy did not look convinced. "Well, Allison, you just take your time and get things settled. You're welcome any time. Lord knows we ain't going anywhere."

"Thank you, Nancy. I appreciate your patience. I promise to come by just as soon as we get things settled. Have you had any new arrivals since I saw you?"

Nancy shook her head sadly. "No, and it seems to me that even the casual lookers have dried up. Folks just aren't buying. I used to see people walking around gawking all the time; now the place is deserted. God knows when I'm going to get any actual neighbors. You know what I think? I think people are scared to come here, or at least are waiting for the whole Invisible Man thing to blow over."

"Has anyone said that?"

"Not to me, but a person can't help but be spooked by all this mysterious killing going on. I tell you, Allison, the sooner they catch this guy, he better it will be for all of us."

"Amen to that," said Allison.

"So, anyway, how's the article coming?"

"I'm writing on the hidden side of Florida. You know; the part the tourists seldom see. The crackers in the back country, the crocodile wranglers, the shrimp fishermen, the Flagler hotels, and all the quirky things that make Florida unique."

Nancy looked at her curiously. "You want the hidden side of Florida? Well, I happen to know an old Haitian woman who sometimes comes around Davis Shores selling trinkets and jewelry. But that's just a sideline. She has a sort of magic and witchcraft shop in the old town. I stopped by once. It gave me the creeps, but you might like to include it in your article. I could take you there in a few minutes if you'd like."

Allison considered. "Well, it certainly sounds like it would fit in with my article. Sure. Let's go."

The Sheriff's office seemed much busier than Max remembered it. The phone never seemed to stop ringing and several reporters hovered in the background.

"Hey, Max." said Atley. "Looks like I'm the center of attention around here. These press boys are everywhere. I fobbed off my deputy, Buford on them."

"Well, it is a sensational story," said Max. "Listen. I have some information. I found a magazine article with the names and background of all the victims so far, and two who are still alive. I've been wondering how the killer found his victims. I think he was using that same article to select his victims. If that's true, we have the names of his next victims and one of them is D.P. Davis."

"Holy cow. Does Davis know?"

"I just told him. He doesn't want to take any extra precautions. He says it would be hiding."

"So what? If I thought this guy was after me, I'd hide. What about the other one?"

"Calvin Warfield in Melbourne. I already checked. He's at his estate fiddling with his private art collection. Apparently he spends a lot of time there. It seems like a good place for an Invisible Man murder."

"How would the killer arrange that little feat?"

"I don't know, but the smart play is to stop him before he tries. We have two suspects. Can we get their pictures?"

"We have a picture of Carpellini from the Navy and Anderson's wife has supplied one of him. Maybe we can have men guarding them and looking for the suspects if one of them shows up."

"Good," said Max, "but I'd like to look at the place to see if I can figure out what the Invisible Man might be up to. I don't want to depend on recognizing him."

"I'm sure that can be arranged, but what if Davis is the next in line?"

"Maybe you can have a couple of plain clothes men watch him discretely for his own protection, but I think Warfield is the next target. The killer seems to be taking the names in the order they appear in the article except for the first one."

"Russo?"

"Right," said Max. "He was number three in the article but the first murder. That makes me wonder why."

"Search me."

"I'm wondering if the first murder wasn't the critical one," said Max. "Maybe that was the real target because that was the man who did him wrong. That was the one he did first because he wanted to make sure he got him. Then he did the others in the order they appeared in the article."

"How would you find out?"

"I think I'll drop by the Russo Company and see what they have in their files."

"But Max, we already know that both Carpellini and Anderson were customers of Russo."

"Yes, but I'm wondering which one was the most bent on revenge. Maybe the correspondence will show that. Then maybe we'll know which one of our suspects to be on the lookout for."

"Good," said Atley. "I'll start to quietly set up some plain clothes officers to watch Davis and maybe to watch over Warfield's place."

"Good," said Max. "But if the security is too obvious, it might scare our man off and he'll come back when we aren't there."

"I think I can dig up some boys that'll blend in with the wallpaper, Max."

In another part of St Augustine, Nancy led Allison to a narrow street whose monotony was relieved by a single scraggly palm tree. No one seemed to be around except a few idlers sitting on the curb half asleep.

"I don't suppose they hold the debutante's ball around here," said Allison.

"There's a lot of Haitians around here," said Nancy. "Compared to where they came from, this is the Ritz. Ah, here we are."

If anything, the small storefront was even shabbier than the rest of the woe begotten street. There was no sign, and whatever was in the window was only a blur behind the grime. Nancy opened the door and Allison could see a cloud of dust motes dancing in the air.

The warped wooden shelves behind the counter were filled with candles, feathers, dolls, various bottles, and a human skull that Allison hoped wasn't real. Two red candles flickered in the gloom.

As they stood there wondering what most of the items could possibly be for, an ancient black woman, whose face looked as if it had been carved from ebony by a sculptor with shaky hands materialized in the gloom.

"You folks want a charm?" She had a strange accent that seemed a combination of French and some Caribbean island.

"I got charms to make man look at you, and charm to make you well if you sick. I got charm to help you have baby."

Allison started when she heard that one.

"I was telling my friend here about your shop," said Nancy. "She is writing a magazine article about the hidden side of Florida, so I thought your shop would be perfect."

The woman was not impressed. "Shop not hidden. Shop right on de street."

"What is in those bottles?" Allison asked.

"Dey be potions; potions what help you in life or potions to help you find t'ings or potions to help you kill an enemy."

"I don't think I need that one," said Allison.

"Let me see your hand, lady," the woman said, and took Allison's hand and passed a long feather over it. "Ahhhh, you be wanting baby I think."

"What? How do you...I mean..."

"I have medicine get you baby. You want boy or girl?"

"Well..."

The woman took a few colored beans and placed them in a bag. "You take dese beans and you smash them up. You mix in tea when the moon be full. You get baby. One dollar."

"Well, in the interests of journalism..." Allison paid the shopkeeper.

"If I may ask, what sort of a shop is this? Are you some sort of VooDoo person?"

"VooDoo? Really Allison." Nancy was shocked.

"Nancy I don't think this lady is exactly a Presbyterian."

"I am a Bokor," the woman said in a softer voice. "Bokor serve Loa spirits. Loa spirits serve Bondye. Loa are like your saints and Bondye is big God."

Allison had her trusty pad out and was writing furiously. "Do the Loa have names like the saints?"

"Sure. Papa Legba, Simbi, Baron Samedi, and Erzulie. Many more."

"And where are these Loa? Around here?"

The woman leaned over and looked at her with watery brown eyes lined in yellow with red veins. "Loa are spirits. Loa everywhere. See everything. You use beans. You see. Erzulie help you get pregnant."

Allison thanked the woman and left with Nancy, still clutching her small bag of beans. She noticed that her palms were sweating, even though it was a cool day.

Chapter 25
Letters

Back at the Alcazar an hour later, Max put down the lobby phone.

"Well. I just talked to D.P. Davis again to urge him to take some precautions, since his name is on the list."

"What was his reaction?" said Allison.

"Let's just say that if the killer decides to tangle with D.P. he might be sorry. Davis already feels put upon by the economy. He just regards the Invisible Man as the last straw. Anyway, based on how it's gone so far, the killer will follow the names in the order they appeared in the article. That means he'll focus on Calvin Warfield next."

"I wouldn't rely on that. The killer seems to be pretty slippery."

"That he is. So what's all this about you visiting some sort of Voodoo magic shop today? Is that a hidden side of Florida?"

"It was sure hidden to me."

"And this is the woman who invited us to dinner at Davis Shores?"

"That's right."

"I wonder what will be on the menu? Eye of newt with a side order of toe of frog?"

As they made their way back to the room, Allison told Max about her trip to the Voodoo shop.

"So she gave you some magic beans for pregnancy, did she?" said Max. "Sounds like Jack and the Beanstalk. She must be a little rusty on her biology."

"Oh, I know it's silly, but standing in that shop with all the totems and candles around..."

"Exactly. They use props and atmosphere to put the reasoning power to sleep."

"I know, but a lot of people believe in it, Max. Besides, you remember that spiritualist I was about to expose up in Easton a couple of years back? She was a fraud and admitted it, but she gave comfort to a lot of people who couldn't find it any other way. Maybe this lady does the same thing."

"Maybe," Max agreed. "After all, Voodoo has been around for a long time. It must have something going for it."

"But, Max, how did she know I wanted to have a baby? I never said anything about the Max, Jr project."

"Well, if I had a shop like that and a woman about your age came in with a friend, I'd assume she has no children at home or she wouldn't have time to be gallivanting around town with a girlfriend. So we have a childless woman in her twenties wearing a wedding ring. Assuming she was at least thinking about having a baby would be a pretty logical guess."

"Hmmm," said Allison. "Looks like you're not the only detective in St Augustine. That lady could give Sherlock Holmes some lessons in deduction."

"I guess we won't be needing the beans then," Allison said as they got into bed a little later..

"I guess not."

"Good. I like the old way better, anyhow."

At the Sheriff's office the next morning, Atley was looking more harassed than ever.

"I tell you, Max, if the Task Force had any chance to do any real police work, the boys from the press have put the kibosh on it. They're everywhere and asking more damn fool questions..."

"Have you been talking to them?"

"No, but the governor has this aide who can't keep his mouth shut. He keeps talking about how we're mobilizing and committing resources and the like. Trouble is, when they pinned him down, he admitted we didn't have the killer's name yet and we weren't sure just how he pulled off his crimes. I just can't wait for that to get in the papers."

"Actually," said Max, thinking about it, "it might not be a bad idea if we made the Invisible Man think we were in the dark. It might make him careless."

"How do you mean, Max?"

"Well, if he knew we were looking for a car with a Virginia license plate, for instance, he might steal some local plates and substitute them, but if he thought we didn't know about the plates, he might just go right on driving around with them showing."

Atley nodded. "He might at that. Yeah, I guess it's better that he knows too little about what we're doing than too much."

"Speaking of which," said Max. "Is there any news about our suspects?"

"Yes!" Atley waved telegram in the air. "I just got this about a half hour ago. Carpellini is our man! Anderson showed up from his latest traveling salesman jaunt and it turns out he has a broken arm with a plaster cast all the way past the elbow. The man can barely drive an automobile, so he couldn't have dragged that canoe, or paddled it. He'd have had a hard time overpowering Russo with only one good arm as well. No; that lets him out."

"Did they check?" Max asked.

"Yep. They checked with the doctor and with the hospital that set his arm. He had a compound fracture and the cast has been on for over a month. No, there's no doubt. He couldn't have done it. Carpellini's our man."

Max nodded. "Well, that does fit in with the gold ring with the anchor on it."

"We have a picture of Carpellini, but I don't think it'll be much help. First of all, according to your interview with the canoe guy and our interview with the marina guy at Lake George, Carpellini wears dark glasses and a hat pulled down over his hair. But even without that, he looks pretty ordinary according to the picture, so it isn't likely anyone would recognize him anyway."

"Probably not" said Max. "Well, I suppose it's just a matter of finding this guy, but still..."

"Still what?"

"Carpellini just doesn't seem like a good candidate. The killer is planning carefully to both make a big splash and to not get caught."

"So?"

"So why start by going AWOL? If that's part of his plan, he'll be in hiding the rest of his life. Desertion is asking for trouble; it doesn't seem like something a meticulous planner would do. Even if he gets away with the murders, he could wind up in the brig for desertion. No one could be that mad at a real estate developer to jeopardize himself that way. Then there's the matter of the first murder. That still bothers me."

"Not as much as it bothered Russo," Atley quipped, "but what's the problem?"

"All the murders were carefully planned and the victims had no chance to resist, but in the first murder, the killer used a knife against a victim with a gun. That couldn't have been in the plan. It just seems so unlikely. I'm betting the killer had no idea Russo had a gun until he was looking down the barrel."

Atley scratched his chin. "Well, you know what Sherlock Holmes would say. 'Once you have eliminated that which is impossible, what remains, however improbable, must be the truth'. And that is what we've done."

Max raised his eyebrows. "I'm impressed. You're a man of refined literary tastes."

"Damn right."

"In this case, however, I have to respectfully disagree with the Mr. Holmes. That axiom assumes complete knowledge; it assumes that there is no information we do not have and did not consider. Unfortunately, that is never the case. You can't know everything and too often, you don't know enough. What you don't know *can* hurt you."

"Well, you can hold out for Jack the Ripper if you want to, Max, but as far as I'm concerned, Carpellini is our man."

"So have you contacted Mr. Warfield to set up police protection?"

Atley lit a cigarette and shook his head. "We tried, but Warfield isn't cooperating. He says he won't have police milling around in his home, even plainclothes ones. That's the trouble with these tycoons; they tend to be rugged individualists at the worst possible times."

"Anyway, he says he keeps a gun in his desk and he won't have a policeman in his house."

"Russo had a gun too. How about a plainclothes man or two?"

"No. The best we'll be able to do is set up surveillance just outside the property."

"Maybe if you went down and talked to him?"

"No dice. He says no police, period."

Max nodded. "At least he's consistent. What if I go down and see him? I'm not a cop, and even if I can't convince him, maybe I can see what the setup is and help plan the surveillance."

"It's worth a try," said Atley. "Here's his address and telephone. Meanwhile, I'll be looking for Carpellini. Say, what about Russo's office? Are you still planning on going there?"

"Maybe when I get back," said Max. "This is more important."

Back at the hotel, Allison settled back in a lobby sofa organizing her notes and continuing her article.

Florida: It's not what you think
The hidden sides of the Sunshine State
By Allison Hurlock
(continued)

Florida is more than hot sun and hotter real estate. Beyond the beaches and the sunburned tourists is an amazingly complex world. In Florida, cowboys heard cattle in the swamps, hunters stalk massive alligators in the Everglades, men work as debt slaves in Turpentine camps, land barons dine in luxurious hotels, farmers plant hundreds of acres of orange groves, entire communities still speak Spanish, Seminole Indians live in isolated areas, both black and white bootleggers mix hell-brew in dark woods, major league baseball teams come here for spring training, the Ringling Brothers Circus is considering coming here for the winter, Portuguese sponge divers harvest the waters off Tarpon Springs, and VooDoo devotees sell charms on dusty side streets. Even if it had cold weather and no beaches, Florida would still be one of the most fascinating states in the Union.

Most visitors and retirees only experience the surface of Florida, never suspecting the depths and complexities of this unique state. Florida's past is colorful and eventful enough, but its present is nothing short of fascinating.

"Allison, how grand to see you again!"

She looked up and saw Julian DeKuyper standing nearby. This time he was wearing a tan suit, but he still sported the white Panama hat.

"Why, hello Julian. You seem to pop up everywhere I go. Is that planned?"

"That is merely fate, or perhaps Kismet as they say in the desert. I am here on a mission."

"A mission? What sort of mission?"

"A mission to help you and your husband."

"Help us? What do you mean?"

He sat down next to her on the sofa, a little closer than she would have preferred.

"I was at the Zorayda last night again. Oh, you would have loved it. They had a new band and the joint was jumping. The mayor was there and feeling no pain, I assure you. Why, at one point..."

"Speaking of points," Allison interrupted, "I do hope you are getting to one."

"Oh, I am indeed. Well, it seems I was having a little chat with the bartender. You know, the same one your husband was questioning the other night."

"And?"

"And he remembered something else the mysterious man with the signet said, something he forgot to tell your husband."

"And what was that?"

DeKuyper squeezed closer and lowered his voice.

"It seems that at one point, the mysterious man said that the real estate people who had mislead the gullible public would answer for their crimes and that they would do so in the most sensational way possible, just so the rest of them got the message. I heard from another source that the man in question walks with a limp."

"Are you sure about this, Julian?"

"I told you I have my sources, Allison, and you can be sure I will continue to use them and let you know what I find out."

Allison looked at him curiously. "Julian, when you tried to sell us real estate at the Zorayda, I thought I finally had you figured out."

"And now?" he smiled.

"And now I think you might be selling something else entirely."

"What would that be?"

She shook her head slowly. "I wish I knew."

The Warfield house was at the end of a modest looking driveway outside of Melbourne. Max arrived a little after one and was welcomed by the housekeeper, an elderly lady with watery eyes.

"Mr. Warfield is in the gallery, Mr. Hurlock. This way." She led Max to a large wooden door and opened it.

The gallery proved to be a large room addition off the main corridor. It had high ceilings and was cluttered with paintings, sculptures, several Egyptian items including a mummy case and a desk in the center. On the desk was a pitcher of some liquid, a pair of large glasses, and an ice bucket. Behind the desk was a bald man dressed in dark brown and sporting a gray beard.

"So you're Hurlock, are you? Well, I agreed to see you as a courtesy to the police, but if you ask me, it's a lot of damned foolishness. But you're here, so have a seat."

Max sat.

"Thank you for seeing me on such short notice, Mr. Warfield. I know you're a busy man."

'That's right. I usually spend most of my time at the office, but Tuesday is my day to visit art galleries, and today is my day to catalogue my collection and to review catalogues for future purchases, so I would appreciate it if you would be brief."

"Fair enough," said Max. "As you know, a killer is going around the state murdering leaders of the real estate industry. We have reason to believe you may be next on his list. The police are tracking down this man, but until they nab him, they believe you need some extra protection."

"I understand all that, Mr. Hurlock, but I am a man of certain fixed habits. I have reached the stage in life where I value both my routine and my privacy. I will not have a team of flatfoots roaming around my house and grounds. I know you mean well, but I have all the protection I need right here."

Warfield slid open a drawer and pulled out a .45 Colt pistol and placed it on the desk with a thud.

"When I am at home I spend most of my time in here. If anyone comes in that door bent on mayhem, he is very likely to get lead poisoning."

Max nodded and looked around. "This is certainly an impressive collection. My wife writes articles for magazines and she recently did one on private museums. She'll be sorry she missed this one."

Warfield perked up. "I read that article. Is your wife Alice Hurlock?"

"Allison, but yes. Did you like the article?"

"A little superficial for real collectors, but a sound effort overall. I could tell her a thing or two about private collections. You must bring your wife to my reception Sunday. We can have a good chat. Maybe she can feature my little museum in a future article."

"Did you say reception?"

"Yes. I'm having a reception here for everyone living at Warfield Commons. That's my development just south of Melbourne. I do it every year as a sort of thank you, and to announce anything new. The people appreciate it and it keeps me in touch."

"Mr. Warfield, under the circumstances, I'm not sure that's a good idea. There's a killer running around out there and that'll just paint a big bulls eye on your back."

"Nonsense. I have to go about my business. Besides, I've already announced it in the local newspapers and in mailings to investors."

"...mailings to investors," Max repeated. "I would really recommend you reconsider."

"Out of the question."

"Well then at least allow the police to station a few men around for your protection. They can be plainclothes and blend in with the guests."

"Oh, all right. If you really think it's best, but they'd better stay out of the way."

"I'm sure they will," said Max, hoping he was right.

"Done. Now the doors open at noon. There's an open bar and I usually come out of the gallery around twelve thirty to greet everyone. If you bring Allison, I think I can guarantee you a personal tour beforehand."

"Who will be here besides the guests and the bartender?" Max asked. "Any security people?"

"The caterer is coming to set up in the dining room around ten and there will be a cleaning crew around eleven. Otherwise, nobody except the plainclothes people you talked me into."

"I guess that will have to be enough," said Max. "At least, let's hope so."

Max stopped back at the Sheriff's office and told Atley what had happened.

"All right, Max. I'll arrange for six plain clothes guys to be there Sunday. Are you and Allison going?"

"I'm planning on it. The more eyes on Warfield the better. This is the only victim where we've had advanced warning."

"So are you still going to check the files at Russo's office?"

"Tomorrow. Tonight I have a date for dinner at Davis Shores."

Two hours later, they were on the Davis Shores ferry that D.P. Davis had made available. The sun was going down and the water was calm. Long ripples spread out in the boat's wake.

"Max, I'm so glad we could come tonight, I'm anxious for you to meet Nancy and Bill. Besides, you need a break from the investigation grind."

"I don't need a break; I need a solution, but I'm going tonight on your recommendation."

"So Max, do you still think the police might be chasing the wrong man?"

"Not necessarily. It's just that from what I know of Mario Carpellini, he seems to be a pretty lukewarm candidate. Still, people fool you, I suppose. I'm going to Russo's office to look through the correspondence files tomorrow to see if I can find anything more, but mostly to reassure myself. It just doesn't all fit together as well as I'd like. I just feel like I've been a step behind for weeks. I can't seem to bring anything to a conclusion. First they asked me to find Bubba back in Maryland and I couldn't find Bubba. Then Glenn Curtiss himself asked me to find the Invisible Man and I haven't been able to do that either. I'm starting to think I couldn't find an elephant in a circus."

"I have faith in you, Max. Was that little tidbit I heard from Julian DeKuyper today any help?"

"Not really, even assuming it was true."

"What do you mean?"

"Allison, has it occurred to you that Mr. DeKuyper might have, well, embellished that tale simply to have an excuse to get close to you?"

"I considered it. It was a pretty innocuous piece of information, true or not."

"Well, here we are at the dock. It looks like their house is a block or so that way."

The house was Spanish style with stucco walls and a red tile roof. It stood alone on a newly paved street with a few trees and shrubs gamely struggling to survive.

"What did you say her last name was?" Max asked as the approached the front door.

"You know, she never said. It was always just Nancy. I never told her my last name either. Things tend to be informal at Davis Shores it seems. She was glad just to have someone to talk to."

The door opened and Nancy gushed a greeting.

"Allison. I'm so glad you could finally make it."

"Nancy, this is my husband, Max."

"Hi, Max. I've been having a great time with Allison."

"Me, too," said Max.

"I hope you don't mind, but I made meatloaf instead of Jambalaya. It seems Bill forgot to bring home some shrimp."

"No problem," said Allison. "That will be a taste of home."

Nancy turned and hollered towards a back room. "Hey, Bill. Allison is here with her husband!"

In a few seconds, Bill appeared in the doorway and his mouth dropped open.

"Max?"

"Bubba?"

For once, Allison could think of nothing to say.

John Reisinger

Chapter 26
Ghosts from the past

"Oh, my God," said Nancy after a moment of stunned silence. "Nobody down here ever calls him Bubba. You guys know each other?"

"Nancy, I went to school with Max here. I ain't seen him since before the war."

"So you don't go by Bubba anymore?" Allison asked.

"Naw. Nancy says Bill is more respectable."

"Come on in to dinner, everyone," said Nancy. "I have a feeling there will be a lot to talk about."

Nancy's meatloaf was giving off delicious odors and making everyone even hungrier than they already were.

"Do you cook meatloaf, Allison?" Nancy asked politely.

"I did once," Allison answered, "until the St Michaels Volunteer Fire Department asked me to stop. I'm afraid my cooking skills are still developing."

"So Bubba," Max interrupted. "Do I have to ask?"

"Ask what?"

"What are you doing here? People up in Annapolis and the shore are looking for you. They asked me to find you, but I hit a dead end. What happened?"

Bubba leaned back and prepared to expound, a pose Max had seen him take many times in the past. "Well Max. My buy boat business didn't do too well. Oh, I had a couple of good years, in fact, we bought this lot as an investment during one of 'em. But most times the expenses were always bigger than the income. I owed money to everybody and the bank was breathing down my neck about a bounced check. Then one day Nancy saw an article about people moving to Florida and it sure sounded nice. I had just gotten home from a bad trip on the bay in January. My nose was red, my fingers were numb, and I had a coating of ice all over my back. I was wet, cold and miserable. Well sir, that's all it took. We decided to leave the boat and build a house on that Florida lot and here we are. Mr. Davis was so happy we were going to be living here that he gave me a job driving one of the Davis Shores ferries. Nancy got a part time job as a secretary in town and here we are. We didn't mean to worry anybody, we just needed to start over."

"Well, Max," said Allison. "Looks like your luck in finding people is changing."

"Let's hope it continues."

"The dinner was as delicious as it smelled and the four got on as if everyone had been friends for years. Nancy and Allison joked about the Voodoo shop and Max and Bubba reminisced about high school. After desert, Nancy's almost-famous rice pudding, the talk drifted in the direction of current events in Florida and that meant the Invisible Man.

"I heard about that no-good,' said Bubba. "And I heard about the cases you been solving, Max. I always knew you had it in you. Allison, did you know that Max once saved my life? Well, not really, but almost. Somebody stole the teacher's purse right out from her desk. It was supposed to be a joke, but she wasn't laughing. Naturally, she blamed me, but Max worked out this time schedule that proved the purse was taken when I was at the principal's office for something else. Turned out Bobby Preston took it."

"It was nothing," said Max.

"Anyway," Bubba continued. "I ain't no detective or anything, but I've been thinking about this Invisible Man guy, and I got an opinion. You want to hear it?"

Max really didn't, but said he did.

"Well, do you remember that time I was the hall monitor?"

"Remember it? We referred to that period as the 'Reign of Terror.'".

"I guess I let the responsibility and the power go to my head a little."

"A little," Max agreed.

"Anyway, thinking about it, it seems to me that this killer might be having the same problem."

"Uh...I'm not sure I'm following you, Bubba."

Bubba leaned forward and gestured, something he often did when he was trying to be serious. "At first I was real careful and cautious about everything, but the more I did, the more I wanted to do and the less I thought about it. I got confident, then I got overconfident. I was in charge for the first time in my life and I got carried away."

"I remember. But what does that have to do with the killer?"

"Well, he's been at this for a while now, and he's gotten away with it. The newspapers talk about him and people act as if he's supernatural. I'm thinking maybe he's letting it go to his head too. I bet he's getting careless and sloppy. Maybe he's been building his confidence and now he's overconfident and he's taking more chances and doing riskier things because he's always been successful and thinks he's bullet proof. And that means he just might be ripe for the pickin'. And just maybe, Max, you'll be the one doin' the picking."

Much later, when the ferry had deposited Max and Allison back in St Augustine and they walked back to the Alcazar, Allison leaned her head on Max's shoulder.

"So that was the famous Bubba. I must say I half expected a cow to come strolling into the living room."

"Maybe Bubba's reformed. He's still a little frayed at the edges, though."

"What about that idea that the Invisible Man might be getting careless because of hubris? Do you think Bubba's right? Could the killer be taking bigger risks to top himself?"

"I've been thinking about that since the elevator murder," said Max. "Bubba might be right. Each murder is a little riskier than the last. The first murder was in an otherwise empty building with no witnesses; the next was on a lake in the open, though also with few possible witnesses; the elevator murder was in a building with witnesses on every other floor and the possibility of someone seeing the killer come or go; and the murder in the tree was in the woods during hunting season, with other hunters all over. Yes, I think Bubba's right. The Invisible Man is getting more confident and is taking more risks to create his effects. Let's hope the next risk is big enough to be his downfall."

"So Bubba confirmed what you were already thinking?"

"More or less, but I value his opinion, because he has firsthand experience."

"Not only that," said Allison, "but finding Bubba taught us an important lesson tonight."

"What lesson is that?"

"Your luck is changing. You've started to find what you set out to find. Against all the odds, you found Bubba. Can the Invisible Man be far behind?"

At the same moment, some miles away, the Invisible Man was regarding a newspaper story with satisfaction.

POLICE BAFFLED IN REALTOR DEATHS
INVISIBLE MAN REMAINS ELUSIVE

A spokesman for the Governor's Special Task Force charged with apprehending the so-called Invisible Man today admitted that authorities are still baffled by both the identity of the killer and the means by which he is carrying out his crimes, that have so far claimed the lives of four Florida real estate men.

"We are mobilizing our resources and expanding the assets that are committed to this case," said aide Norman Collison. But when asked about the specifics of the state's progress, Collison said "No, we haven't arrested a suspect yet; we're still working on figuring out the killer's methodology."

Local citizens, especially those connected with the real estate industry, are demanding faster action by the state authorities.

"I pay my taxes to this state," said Jacksonville real estate agent Jack Duffy, "so I think the least they could do would be to keep me from being murdered in my sleep. They should have had this guy in jail a month ago."

The Invisible Man carefully folded the paper and put it with the others. He was getting an impressive collection of articles about the murders.

He then laid out the items he had assembled on a table for inspection. First, there was the tan jacket. It looked good and it seemed to fit well either way it was worn. Reversible garments often didn't, so he was glad he had spent a little more on it. Then there was his .38 pistol; a revolver; reliable and with the additional advantage of not leaving shell casings behind. He had a silencer for it, but this time, would not use it. The loud gunshot noises and the reaction they would cause were part of the plan. He counted out five cartridges and loaded the pistol, leaving one chamber empty beneath the hammer. This would prevent the possibility of an accidental discharge. Besides, five cartridges would be three more than he would need.

He then placed the box from the theatrical supply house on the table, opened it, and examined its contents. Yes, that would do nicely; very nicely indeed.

Having inspected the items, the Invisible Man walked into the bathroom and started to cut his hair.

Chapter 27
Letters

Max drove up to the Russo company the next morning. The office manager was happy to see him and offered whatever help he could.

"Yes, of course you can see the correspondence files. We have the files in these cabinets outside of Mr. Russo's office."

"Do you keep a separate file for letters from people complaining?"

"No, we just file them by date under general correspondence."

Max took the first batch of correspondence files dated six months before the first murder and began to go through it. The files consisted of both original letters and carbon copies of outgoing correspondence. He skipped over the carbons and looked at what came in. After an hour, he sat back and stretched.

"Whew! There is sure a lot of dull correspondence in a real estate sales office."

Max stood up and walked out into the main office to stretch his legs. Several workers looked at him curiously.

"Are the police making any progress?" one man asked.

"They're grinding away," said Max. "They have some leads they are looking at."

"Do they still think it was an unhappy customer?"

Max nodded. "That's the theory."

"Well, we've had a few of those, but I never heard of anybody threatening to kill anyone."

Max went back and resumed the search. Soon, he came upon several letters addressed to Mr. Russo expressing dissatisfaction with some aspect of a transaction and complaining that the resale possibilities were slim. Russo's sympathetic and businesslike answers were also in the file. None of these letters seemed threatening, simply unhappy.

Max also found the letters from both Anderson and Carpellini, the last two suspects, although it would seem that Anderson had just been eliminated. Anderson's letter was a little more aggressive than the others, and threatened "serious consequences" if things didn't improve. Carpellini's letter called Russo a crook and gave him one month to return Carpellini's money or there would be trouble. These letters were noticeably more threatening than the others, so it was clear why both of these men were suspects. Even so, neither letter provided any new detail or insight.

He plowed on and the story was the same; a scattering of complaints, but only two that could be considered threatening. Of course, someone might have been unhappy but never written at all, but a warning letter seemed more likely.

Finally, Max pulled out a letter from someone named Albert Nyborg, of Brattleboro, Vermont. Nyborg's letter sounded similar to the others in its litany of complaints, but it was the ending that got Max's attention.

"Mr. Russo, I bought these properties in good faith as a means of assuring financial security for my family. You encouraged that view, even though you knew the market for resales was weakening. Now I

have properties I can't use and can't resell without a ruinous loss. All my life savings have gone into the down payment and the monthly payments, and it still isn't enough. I am now facing foreclosure and financial ruin. You mark my words, Mr. Russo; if I don't find a way of making this right, someone is going to die!"

Max read the last line again. "...someone is going to die!" This was more threatening and specific than the letter of the remaining suspect. Why hadn't he heard of Nyborg before? Apparently the name was eliminated from the earlier list for some reason. Maybe he had an alibi. If so, how closely had they really checked out that alibi? Or maybe they had just missed him. He certainly sounded a lot more dangerous than Carpellini. Maybe they should take a second look.

Max asked a secretary to type a duplicate of the letter for him to take back and he left the office. On his way out, he looked back at the small office where Russo had been murdered.

It was still empty.

Back in St Augustine, Atley was waiting for him.

"Max! I've been trying to get ahold of you. It's over! The case is solved! They found Carpellini. And get this; he was in a Tin Can Tourist camp near Gainsville; a perfect jumping off place to carry out the murders."

Max sat in the nearest chair. "They arrested him? When?"

"About an hour ago. They got a tip about a Navy deserter living in a cabin at the camp and the local cops nabbed him."

"I don't suppose he's confessed," said Max.

"Not yet, but they're working on it. He denies everything; says he fell in love with Florida after his ship put in at Miami a couple of years ago. That's why he bought the lot. Then when he got tired of the Navy, he skedaddled."

"He doesn't exactly sound like a mastermind. I suppose he has an automobile?"

"Yup, a Chevrolet, complete with Virginia license plates, just like your canoe seller said."

"All he said was that the name started with V," Max corrected.

"Oh, yes," Atley retorted. "So do the Virgin Islands or Venezuela, but I'd put my money on Virginia. Anyway, Carpellini isn't from Virginia originally, but his ship was stationed in Norfolk, so that's where his auto is registered."

"All right, all right. I take your point. Does he know why he was arrested?"

"Sure, and he admits writing a couple of nasty letters, but says that's as far as it got. But he's our man; no doubt about it. He even had the magazine with the article about the real estate tycoons in his tent."

"So what happens now?"

"Well, Max, if you'll give me the name of that man who sold the canoe, I can get him and Ed the Lake George Marina owner to see if either one of them can pick Mr. Carpellini out of a lineup. I'm not real optimistic, since they both said he was wearing dark glasses and a hat. Still, we went through a lot of names and we finally got him."

"Congratulations, I guess," said Max. "Look, I don't want to be an ant at this picnic, but I found this threatening letter to Russo in his files. I know you just arrested Carpellini, but I wonder why this other guy was eliminated as a suspect. What was his alibi?"

"His alibi? Geez Louise, Max. Does it matter?"

"It matters to me. Could you check the file information on Albert Nyborg?"

"Max, for the love of..."

"Just humor me, would you?"

Atley let out a sigh that sounded like a buffalo pulling his foot out of the mud, then ambled over to the files mumbling to himself. He returned in a few seconds with a manila folder.

"Here it is; Albert Nyborg of Brattleboro, Vermont. A very unhappy customer of the late Mr. Russo, just as you said. Wrote several nasty and threatening letters. Apparently he provided no alibi for his whereabouts during any of the murders."

"No alibi?" said Max. "A guy writes nasty and threatening letters to the first victim and he was eliminated? Why was he dismissed as a suspect?"

Atley turned a page in the file.

"Because he's dead."

John Reisinger

Chapter 28
Various methods

Atley continued to read the file as Max sat silent with disappointment. "And before you ask, Max, he isn't just hiding somewhere and playing dead while he kills people. The investigators verified the death and saw the obituary, death certificate, and the gravesite. There is absolutely no doubt. What's more, Nyborg died weeks before the first murder."

Max ran his fingers through his hair. "Well, I guess that settles it. Nyborg looked like a good lead, but clearly he is not our killer."

"Come on Max. We have the guy in custody. It's over. The forces of law and order have triumphed. Enjoy it."

"I hope you're right, but I'm still uneasy. What if Warfield is next on the list?"

"So what? Carpellini can't get to him if he's in jail and you can bet that no judge is going to grant this guy bail. Warfield is safe. I've already cancelled the plainclothes police guard."

"You what?"

"Be reasonable, Max. I can't spend the taxpayer's money to protect a man who no longer needs it. We've expended too many resources on this case as it is."

"One day? Just to play it safe? How much can that cost? You're tossing dice with a man's life."

"You'll be there, right? You can keep an eye on Warfield."

"You were going to have six plainclothes men there. I am one person and I'm not a cop. I have no authority or powers of arrest. Officially, I don't even exist."

"All right, Max. I'll tell you what. I'll deputize you. Then if another killer shows up, you can arrest him. How's that?"

"Roy G., I have been to that house. One person can't possibly cover it against a killer as careful and determined as the Invisible Man."

"Max, I can't send those men and that's all there is to it. You know what I think? I think you're so used to finding the killer in these cases, that when someone else does, you just can't admit it. Looks like Max Hurlock has an ego after all."

"What? That's bushwa and you know it!"

"All I know is that we caught the Invisible Man and there are only two guys who aren't happy about it; the Invisible Man and my esteemed expert from up north."

Max counted to ten. "All right. If I'm to be the only one looking after Warfield, so be it. Meanwhile, let me use the phone. I think I'd better let Glenn Curtiss know what's going on."

"You know where to find it."

Curtiss was ecstatic. "Great work, Max. I knew you could do it."

"I really didn't do that much," said Max. "It was just good police work, tracking down leads."

"Well, we knew they'd have the credit, no matter how it worked. The important thing is that the case is solved."

"Actually, Glenn, I'm not really certain that it is."

"What? Are you saying they have the wrong man?"

"I'm saying that there are certain inconsistencies with Mario Carpellini being the killer."

He recounted some of the things he had found out and some of his misgivings. There was long pause on the other end of the line. Finally, Curtiss spoke again.

"Max, are you sure about this?"

"I'm not certain, but I have strong doubts. I think Warfield may have been the next target, and if the killer is still out there, Warfield is in real danger. I'm going to a reception at his house Sunday and keep an eye on him."

"All right, Max. Maybe that will put your mind at ease. Meanwhile, I'll be hoping you're wrong."

Max went for a long walk before returning to the hotel. He passed several advertising signs for Florida land, some of them old and tattered. People in the streets scurried about on missions, or walked lazily ogling the architecture and the scenery. Max felt as if he were the only person in St Augustine with a care in the world. The late editions of the newspapers were coming out with screaming headlines such as INVISIBLE MAN CAUGHT, and ARREST IN REALTOR KILLINGS. In the local bars and street corners, small groups of people talked excitedly about the sensational news. Was Atley right? Was he just unhappy that the police has found the killer before he could?

Max and Allison went to dinner at a small barbeque place Max had spotted on his walk earlier. They ordered back ribs and pulled pork. As they waited for their order to arrive, Max recounted the day's events. Allison listened carefully, asked several pointed questions, them frowned in thought.

"So several police departments went through this long process of elimination with disgruntled people who had bought real estate from the victims and felt they had been cheated."

"That's right."

"And the result was to narrow the list of suspects down to one; this Carpellini person, who deserted from the Navy a few weeks before the first murder."

"That is also correct."

"And one witness said the possible killer wears a signet ring with an anchor on it?"

"Yes."

"And this Carpellini was in Florida at the time?"

"Yes."

"And was living at a tourist camp that is located close to the center of the area of the murders?"

"Yes."

"And has a grudge against at least the first person killed?"

"Yes."

"And drives an automobile with a Virginia license plate, just as the canoe seller claimed?"

"Yes."

"But you're uneasy because you found another candidate, a man who died before the first murder even happened. Have I missed anything?"

"No. I think you covered it succinctly."

"I see."

"So what do you think?"

"I think our order is here. Mmmm. It smells great. Dig in, Max. There's nothing like pork to stimulate the brain cells."

"You're not getting off that easily, Allison. Spill it. What do you think?"

Allison took a bite of pulled pork and chewed thoughtfully for a few seconds.

"Max, you know I have great faith in you and your abilities."

"I can feel a 'but' coming."

"Not at all, Max. I was about to say that what I think really doesn't matter. When you have doubts like this, you're usually right. I have to admit I don't see exactly *how* you can be right under the circumstances, but I feel sorry for anyone who bets against you."

"But what do you think? Is Atley right? Am I just unhappy because I didn't finger the killer?"

Allison put down the fork and leaned over the table. "I think that if you believe you're on the right track, then that's the track you need to stay on. You've never been one to go by the consensus and I don't think you should start now."

Max smiled. "You're beautiful when you're bucking me up."

"Oooh. Flattery will get you everywhere. But Max, you're pushing a pretty big stone up a pretty steep hill. Do you know what you're going to do?"

"Well, the most important thing is to somehow keep the killer from adding to his total. Somehow, I have to protect Warfield."

"Isn't that the job of the police?"

"It would be if they believed it was necessary, but since they are convinced they have the killer under lock and key, they see no need for it."

"So there won't be anyone protecting him?"

"Just us."

"Us?"

"Warfield is throwing a sort of open house Sunday afternoon. If the killer is still out there, and if he's still following the list of names in the magazine article. I think that's when he'll strike. Warfield will be looking for you as well."

"Me? Why me?"

"He's a fan of your articles, it seems, especially the one about private museums. He says he wants to show you his gallery."

Allison shrugged. "I guess that's better than showing me his etchings. Count me in."

The clerk at the front desk appeared at their door early the next morning. Max answered the door with fresh shaving cream on his face.

"Telephone call, Mr. Hurlock. It's the sheriff. He says it's important."

Max picked up the telephone in the lobby and heard Atley on the other end. His voice was hesitant and awkward.

"Max, are you coming by today? I need to talk to you, and I wasn't sure...that is..."

"I can come by after breakfast."

Back in the room, Allison was just finished dressing in the red and black dress Max had always liked.

"Ah, you're up," said Max as he entered the room.

"After our, uh activities last night, I was a little tired this morning, she said, but I'm fine now. I may go shopping for a new outfit to wear to the Warfield place. What does one wear to an attempted murder, I wonder?"

"I have to stop by the sheriff's office. How about we meet for lunch?"

"I'd love to, but I'm not sure how long I'll be. I'll see you at dinner. O.K.?"

"See you then."

The sheriff's office was still besieged by reporters interviewing everyone they could find and taking pictures.

"If you think this is bad, you ought to see them up in Jacksonville," said Atley. "That's where they're holding Carpellini. They all want to interview him. Yesterday it was the Florida papers, but today the out of state boys are showing up. I'm heading up there is a few minutes, and I'd sure appreciate it if you could come along."

"Me?" said Max. "You seem to have the situation well in hand without me. Besides, I thought the case was solved."

Atley looked deflated. "Look, Max. I'm sorry I said that stuff about you being unhappy that you didn't finger the killer. I just been under a lot of..."

"Forget it. You say what you think. I do the same thing. Besides, in your place, I might think the same thing. But what's all this about going up to Jacksonville?"

"Well, Max, the truth is that Carpellini isn't cooperating. He's demanding a lawyer and is refusing to answer questions. A fifth amendment cop out! Can you beat that? Why would an innocent man refuse to cooperate?"

Max smiled faintly. "It seems to me that's exactly the kind of man who would refuse to cooperate. Would you cooperate with people who were trying to hang you? I wouldn't, especially if I were innocent."

"All right, Max. I don't need political philosophy right now, I need evidence."

"Better late than never."

"If we want to nail this guy, we have to be able to present a coherent case to a grand jury, but we have a problem."

"I'm listening."

"Well," said Atley awkwardly, "the fact is, we don't really know how he pulled off the murders. I mean, you explained the one on the lake with the canoe that was hidden from view, and I know the killer used that ladder we found to get LaPointe's body up in that tree, but we still can't figure out the others. If Carpellini has a decent lawyer, he can demand we explain how his client was supposed to have done it. The jury might be persuaded to think that if we don't know how the crimes were done then maybe they shouldn't believe we know who did them. Not only that, but the damned reporters are hammering at us all the time to explain how the crimes were done. The public's right to know and all that. We can refuse to discuss it, but we can't admit we don't know."

"I see your dilemma," Max agreed.

"Look, Max. You been pretty tight lipped about it, but I got a feeling you have a pretty good idea of just how the Invisible Man pulled off these crimes. I need to know or the whole case could fall through."

"I'd really like to get the killer to confirm my theories before I speculate."

"Fine. Then come up to Jacksonville and try them on Carpellini."

"Roy G., you just said that Carpellini isn't talking. Besides, I still think he's the wrong guy."

"He isn't talking yet, but if we confront him with that information, it might get him to spill. I want to get charging documents drawn up pronto, so what about it?"

"Let's back up a minute," said Max. "If I tell you my theories, will that suffice? I am not going to Jacksonville today. The Warfield reception is tomorrow and I might be the only thing between him and a bullet. If I show up in Jacksonville with all the excited reporters running around, one of them might latch on to me and make it harder for me to get away to look out for Warfield tomorrow. My name or picture might even show up in an article and tip off the real killer. I can't take the chance."

That's fine, Max, but what about the murders?"

"All right," said Max. "Now, you said you understand about the Godfrey murder on the lake?"

"Right. The Invisible Man bought an old canoe and dragged it into the woods to the shore at a place where Godfrey's boat would prevent anyone at the marina from seeing it. He paddled out and probably asked for help or got close some other way. When Godfrey's back was turned he clubbed him, then, still hidden, he paddled back the way he came and hid the canoe where you found it."

"That's right," Max nodded approvingly. "Pretty obvious when you think about it. And I expect you've figured out how LaPointe ended up draped over a tree limb as well."

"I know they found a ladder a ways away and I know that ladder fit the holes in the ground under the tree. I also know they found a small wooden platform and some ropes nearby. It looked like a tree stand to me."

"That's exactly what it was" said Max "A small portable platform that hunters use to sit in a tree and wait for game. So can you figure out what happened?"

"I guess Carpellini shot LaPointe, then carried the body up the ladder into the tree using the ladder and the tree stand."

"I doubt it," said Max. "Carrying a limp body is hard enough on level ground, but carrying it up a ladder is nearly impossible for most men. Besides, if the ladder had carried all that weight, the depressions in the ground would have been deeper I think. No; LaPointe was already up in the tree on his tree stand, waiting for a deer. The killer shot him from the ground and LaPointe slumped down on the tree stand platform. The killer then climbed the ladder to the platform and wrestled the body on to the adjacent limb. After he climbed down, he took the tree stand and the ladder, and dumped then some distance away, leaving a dead body mysteriously draped on a limb up in a tree."

"Good. How about the elevator?" Atley asked. "I'm really in the dark about that one. The killer obviously wasn't in the elevator with Daniels or he would have been seen getting in or out by witnesses. At first I figured the killer might have shot Daniels when the elevator stopped on the vacant second floor, but that type of elevator wouldn't stop unless it was directed to from inside the cab. The nearest I can figure is the killer installed some kind of mechanical pistol device in the elevator and killed Daniels that way. What I can't figure out is how he aimed it and why we never found it."

"That's an easy one; because it was never there," said Max. "You've been reading too many bad mysteries. There was no mechanical killing device. The real method was much simpler and much more foolproof. You see, you were right the first time. The elevator stopped on the second floor and the killer was waiting. When the doors opened, he shot Daniels with a silenced gun and set the elevator for the fourth floor. It happened so quickly that no one noticed that the elevator took a little longer than usual to make the daily morning journey from the first floor up to the fourth."

"Wait," said Atley, "How do you know this?"

"I first noticed the footprints in the light film of dust on the second floor. The place was vacant and hadn't been cleaned as often as it might have been. Anyway, the prints showed someone came in from the stairwell, then stood around in front of the elevator door for some period of time, then went back to the stairwell again. That was our killer. I also noticed that the body was found in the front of the elevator, by the door, as if Daniels was waiting to get off when the door opened."

"But how did the killer get the elevator to stop on the second floor?"

"He didn't. Daniels stopped it there."

"Daniels? But why would he do that?"

"Because the killer had contacted him a few days earlier and told him he wanted to rent the second floor. The secretary found the record of a phone call from someone they didn't know, and Daniels had a note on his personal calendar about a confidential meeting at nine o'clock. I don't know what the killer's story was exactly, probably an offer to rent the second floor office, but I'm sure it was convincing, and I'm sure he insisted on confidentiality. So Daniels opened the door to his secret meeting and was shot by a silenced gun for his troubles."

"Whew. Now I know why they call you Sherlock Hurlock. But now the big question; what happened in the first murder, the Russo case. How did the killer stab Russo then get out of the locked office while Russo was shooting at him and apparently not get a scratch?"

"Ah, the Russo murder," said Max. "That was the first, the most mysterious, and, in my opinion, the most important. I believe that case set the tone for the others and I believe the killer thought it was the most important as well. That's why it was the first."

"So what do you think happened? How did the killer get in a small locked office and stab Russo to death while Russo was shooting at him at close range?"

"Because that's not what happened."

"What? So what did happen?"

"We'll know more when we nab the killer, but I believe the first killing was never intended to be a spectacular crime at all and did not take place in that locked office."

"Then where..."

"I think the killer went there to confront Russo, and confronted him in the hallway where the drop of blood was found. Maybe he threatened him with the knife, maybe not, but I think Russo, who had reputation for being gruff and unsympathetic didn't respond the way the killer wanted. Maybe he said that the killer just made a bad investment and it was his own fault. Either way, it looks like things escalated and the killer stabbed Russo right there in the hallway."

"Not in the office?"

"No. the killer pulled out the knife and a drop or two of blood fell to the floor from the blade, making the blood stain we found. But Russo's sweater absorbed his blood as he clutched his chest and staggered towards the shelter of his office. The killer was momentarily stunned at what he had done and just stood there immobile for a minute, then he came after the wounded Russo. But by this time, Russo was in his office and digging a pistol out of his desk drawer. Remember that though there was no blood on the floor, there were blood smeared handprints on the desk. Russo fired at the killer and missed, forcing him to retreat. Then Russo locked the office door from the inside. Remember there were blood smears on the door handle. He then staggered back to his desk to phone the police, but lost consciousness and died before he could make the call. The killer, knowing he was now locked out of the office where Russo had sought shelter, and that Russo was armed, panicked and fled. The next day he learned that Russo had died and the papers were talking about how mysterious it all was. And I think that's what gave him the idea of taking his revenge in a series of impossible crimes that would bring his grudge to the world's attention, and would terrorize the ones he didn't kill."

Atley nodded in admiration. "Well, that would certainly account for what we found. I think you've hit on it, Max. I'll confront Carpellini with this and watch him crumble."

"Well, right now I am less interested in those murders than in preventing number five. First thing tomorrow, I'm off to see Warfield."

John Reisinger

Chapter 29
A public reception

The drive to Melbourne the next morning wound through wooded areas, scrub lands, and scatterings of pine and palm trees.

As Max and Allison drove the Packard south, they passed billboards advertising Florida land and tourist camps. Occasionally, they saw roadside stands selling oranges and grapefruits in wooden crates "to take back home". Traffic along the road seemed to consist mostly of automobiles with out-of-state license plates traveling to and from points further south. The day was warm and the sun shone brightly, making cool shadows on the ground. On such a day, the identity of the Invisible Man might have been a mystery, but the great attraction of Florida land surely was not.

Allison leaned back in her seat and took a deep breath of the warm air.

"You know Max, in a few years I don't think we'll recognize this place. It'll be full of tourist towns and new homes."

"Yes, I think the Invisible Man is fighting a war he can't win. The pressures for development are too great. He'll never stop it by just murdering a few people. Florida is changing and that's all there is to it. You might as well try to hold the tide back with a broom."

"So why is he trying? Is it just revenge for losing some money?"

"That's a good question," said Max. "My theory is that everybody gets angry when they think they've been taken advantage of and lost a lot of money. Most

207

people would either calm down eventually or maybe sue someone, but they would get on with life. A very few people, however, simply can't live with the situation. They just burn inside and rage at the injustice of it all. Maybe deep inside, they are embarrassed that they fell for the scam, even if it isn't a scam, but simply bad luck. They can't admit to themselves that they got taken in, or made a costly mistake, so they lash out at others they blame instead. The most dangerous people are those who always are looking for someone else to blame, because from there it's a short step to retribution."

"And you think that's what happened with the Invisible Man?"

"I wouldn't be surprised. None of the usual motives for murder, such jealousy, money, love passions, or power would seem to fit. I don't think the killer is just a homicidal maniac because the murders are too carefully planned. No, I think someone got in too deep with his real estate buying and lost his shirt, so this whole episode is about striking out at someone else. The killer certainly has nothing to gain otherwise."

"It makes sense, but that doesn't really help, does it?"

"No, not much. Well, the reception starts in about an hour, but I want to get there a bit early to get the lay of the land."

"So what are you going to be looking for?"

Max shook his head. "I wish I knew."

The Warfield estate looked much as it had when Max was there a few days earlier, except for the automobiles parked along the drive and on the front lawn. Obviously, this was going to be a big event.

"There must be fifty automobiles here," said Max. "This is one popular place today."

Allison agreed. "Nothing like a free shindig to rustle up the locals to put on the feedbag."

"Not just the locals," said Max. "There are lots of out of state tourists here as well. Look at the license plates; Georgia, Maryland, New Jersey, Virginia...say, that's funny."

"What's that?"

"Do you see that Virginia license plate over there on that blue Nash?"

Allison looked. "Sure; I see it."

"And did you notice where it says the name of the state?"

She took another look. "On the left side, over top of the numbers. So?"

"That places it on the upper left of the plate. But we've been assuming the license plate the canoe seller saw was from Virginia and the prime suspect, Mario Carpellini has a car with a Virginia license plate as well."

"Then it all fits, doesn't it? What's the problem?"

"The problem is that the canoe seller said he saw the letter V on the plate because a lump of mud fell off the *bottom* of it. The letter V on a Virginia plate is on the top."

"True, but he might have been mistaken, Max. You said the plate was covered with mud. How could he be certain where that letter was, especially if the plate had a frame or bracket around it?"

"Possibly. Even so, I think we'll check out the other cars before we go in."

They drove up and down the lines of parked cars. Suddenly Max stopped.

"There." He pointed to a Grey Chevrolet Superior just ahead. "See that yellow plate with the dark green letters and numbers?"

"Vermont."

"Right, but notice where the word Vermont is located."

"On the *bottom, below the numbers.* Max I see what you mean. If the canoe seller was right, that plate had to be from Vermont, not Virginia."

Max nodded. "And under the circumstances, and in view of the relatively small number of Vermont cars in Florida, I'd say there's a good change that car belongs to the Invisible Man. He didn't even bother to put mud over it or use a phony plate because he knows the police have made an arrest and are not looking for him."

"And that means..."

"That means the killer is already in the house! Do you have your note pad?"

"Of course," said Allison, producing it. You want to write down the plate number?"

"As quickly as you can. We have to get to the house before it's too late."

The Warfield house was already crowded and noisy with milling guests when Max and Allison reached the front door. They saw the housekeeper first.

"Where is Mr. Warfield?" said Max.

"Oh, Mr. Hurlock. How good you could come. And this must be your lovely wife. Welcome."

"Where is Mr. Warfield?" Max insisted, looking around anxiously.

"He's in the gallery. It's closed to the guests for another half hour, but he said if you came with your wife, to show you in right away. I think he wants to give her a tour."

"Fine. Thank you," said Max, rushing off with Allison following in his wake.

They passed scores of people walking around and talking in small groups most had drinks or were nibbling plates of food and ogling the décor.

Allison caught up with him as they went down the long hallway towards the gallery.

"Nobody here looks much like a murderer," said Allison.

"No, but one of them probably is."

The gallery was ahead with a sign on the door that said "no admittance".

"How are we going to get in?"

"Warfield told me he never locks it."

To Max's relief, the door handle turned in his grip and the door opened. There, sitting at his desk was Warfield, dressed in his usual dark brown suit. He looked up.

"Ah, Mr. Hurlock; and you've brought your wife. Splendid."

Max shut the door behind them and reached for the latch.

"Mr. Hurlock, what are you doing? I never latch that door unless I'm not at home."

"Mr. Warfield, I believe there is a good chance the Invisible Man is among your guests and intends to kill you."

"Perhaps, but as I told you, I have taken certain precautions." He tapped a pistol lying on his desk. "I can assure you I have taken certain other measures just in case, but I refuse to cower behind a locked door. Now, I would very much like to discuss my collection with...what is your name, my dear?"

"Allison, and as much as I'd love to discuss your collection, I really think you should do as Max says."

"Allison...Max; if this maniac is determined to make an attempt on my life, I would much prefer that he did it in my home where I can take precautions rather than some public place where I can't. Now, don't worry. If any attempt is made, it will be in here where I am alone, not out in the crowd. I assure you, Max, if anyone I don't recognize appears in that doorway, he will be looking down the barrel of my gun before he has a chance to do anything."

"But..."

"I'm sorry, Max, but I have made up my mind. Now how about that tour?"

"I need to use your telephone while you show Allison around."

"Of course. Right here on my desk."

Max dialed the operator a placed a call to the District Attorney's office in Jacksonville and asked for Atley. Atley, who had been questioning Carpellini, came to the phone a minute later..

"Roy G., this is Max. Now listen carefully. I'm down at the Warfield house and I think the Invisible Man is here and will attempt to murder Warfield. How soon can you get some uniforms on the grounds here?"

The exasperation in Atley's voice was clear. "Max, the Invisible Man is here. He's in a jail cell. What are you talking about?"

"I'll bet he hasn't confessed, " said Max.

"Well, not yet. I confronted him with our theories on how the crimes were committed and he didn't crack; all he did was look confused."

"That's because you have the wrong guy and the right guy is here, ready to add Warfield to his list. Now, please, if only as a precaution, how quickly can you get some local police here?"

"By the time I get through to the locals and they round up some men, maybe a half hour or so, but Max, we got the killer already, and just who is supposed to pay for all of this?"

"Look, there's no time to explain, but I think I saw the killer's car. The license is from Vermont, not Virginia."

"Aw, Max, you're not on that Nyborg kick again, are you?"

" Well, Nyborg was from Vermont."

" Nyborg is dead! Did you forget that little detail, Max? How do you figure a dead man can be the killer?"

"I don't know yet; maybe somebody else from Vermont is doing it. Look; here's the license number. Vermont plate, number 12-713. Could you find out who the car is registered to and call me back at this number as soon as you can?"

Atley sighed. "All right, Max. I guess you humored me enough times. I owe you this much."

"Thanks, Roy G....and hurry."

Max hung up the phone and started looking around the gallery for possible hiding places in case the killer was already there. He saw a suit of armor and a mummy case, but they were empty. Nothing else was big enough to conceal even a child.

Max caught up to Warfield and Allison, but didn't listen to what Warfield was saying and he kept his eye on the unlocked door to the hallway.

"Now, Allison and Max, if you will excuse me, I have a few notes to make before I emerge to greet my guests in about twenty minutes. Must keep up the tradition. After all, some local people come every year and I wouldn't want them to think I was shifting things."

"Wouldn't want them to think you were dead, either," Max grumbled on the way out.

Then the telephone on Warfield's desk rang.

"It's some sheriff for you, Max," said Warfield, handing him the telephone. Max picked it up and heard the confused voice of Sheriff Atley.

"Max, what is going on down there? Is this your idea of a joke?"

"You don't hear me laughing, do you?" said Max.

"Well, I got the information back on that license plate, but it doesn't make any sense. Are you sitting down? It's registered in the name of Albert Nyborg of Brattleboro, Vermont."

"What? But how...Wait a minute," said Max, thinking quickly. "I know Albert Nyborg is dead, but how did he die, exactly?"

"Looks like it was a suicide."

"Suicide?"

"Yeah. It seems he was so despondent over his bad Florida land deals he took an overdose of sleeping pills. The investigators checked it out with the hospital."

"Then how did his automobile get down to Florida and who's driving it? Albert Nyborg has to be behind this somehow, but how did..." Max stopped. "Roy G., I have to go. I think I know what's going on, and I have to stop it. Just get the police out here as quickly as you can."

Chapter 30
Chaos at Warfield Hall

As the door shut behind them, Allison turned to Max.

"So does this mean that Nyborg isn't dead after all?"

"Albert Nyborg is dead, all right, but someone is driving his automobile and killing people."

"But who would..."

"Never mind that right now. What's important is that we find him and stop him."

"All right, but how?"

Max looked around at the guests moving about. "I'm going to take a closer look at the guests and see if anything looks unusual, or anyone looks unusually nervous. I will be especially alert for anyone wearing a signet ring, one with an anchor. Why don't you stay where you have a view of the door to the gallery in case anyone starts to head that way."

"And what do I do if someone does?"

"If someone starts to open that door, you scream bloody murder and I'll come running."

"Well, that will liven up the party."

"Not as much as a murder. Just let it rip. I'll do the rest."

For the next ten minutes, Allison watched the doorway and Max circulated among the crowd looking for anyone who looked nervous or otherwise out of place. Everyone seemed normal. They ate and drank and laughed and talked just as anyone would at such an event. Max tried to keep an eye on the gallery door at the same time, but lost sight frequently. Allison, however, kept watch carefully so no one could get in the room unnoticed. Max kept listening for a scream, but there was none. All remained quiet as the minutes passed and he scanned the faces in the crowd. They all looked like people enjoying a free reception. No one looked grim, no one was doing anything suspicious, and no one had a signet ring with an anchor.

Suddenly, Allison was at his elbow.

"Max!"

"Allison, why aren't you watching the door?"

"I was, but I saw something funny. Mr. Warfield went for a quick visit to the hall bathroom, then went back to the gallery."

"Well, I suppose he had a call of nature. There's no bathroom in the gallery."

"But Max, I was watching carefully. I saw him emerge from the bathroom and walk back to the gallery plain as day, but *I never saw him leave the gallery to get to the bathroom in the first place.* The first time I saw him was when he walked out of the bathroom. So how did he get there?"

"Oh, no. Stay here!"

Max rushed down the hallway to the gallery, dodging and pushing people aside as he ran. The gallery door was closed. He reached for his pistol.

Max jerked the gallery door handle and to his horror, found it was bolted from the inside. He started pounding on the door.

"Open up! This is the police!"

By this time everyone in the hallway was looking on curiously. A few were starting to walk towards the commotion.

"Open up!" Max shouted, throwing his weight against the door. From inside two shots exploded. Max threw himself against the door again and heard cracking from the wood. One of the men in the crowd pushed as well and the door burst open.

As the door swung open, Max saw the gallery once more just as it had been, except that Warfield was no longer sitting at the desk. The room appeared to be empty! Then Max heard a groan from behind the desk and rushed to find Warfield on the floor barely conscious. Others were rushing into the room now, and crowding around the desk. Warfield didn't open his eyes. He just weakly mumbled a few words.

"He looked like me. He looked like me."

Max jumped to his feet. Suddenly, he knew what had happened.

The Invisible Man had pulled off a perfect locked room murder.

The gallery was chaos as people filed in from the hall to see what was going on. Max looked around desperately.

And then he heard it.

From somewhere down the hallway, past the crowd in the gallery doorway came a piercing shriek. "Aaaaaaaaaaaaaaaaaa!"

It rose louder and louder until it reached a peak that threatened to crack the windows. Some in the crowd were holding their ears.

Allison.

Max pushed through the crowd and saw Allison standing near the end of the hallway where he had left her. She started to scream again, but stopped when she saw Max emerge from the crush of bodies.

"Max! Hurry! He's getting away! He went out that door towards the parking area."

Max flew through the front door and saw a man in a tan jacket running over the lawn towards the car with the Vermont license plate. In the distance, Max heard sirens.

Max was gaining, but the man had a big head start. He jumped in the car and started the engine. The car had an electric starter.

With wheels spinning in the grass, the car started to move and turned towards the main road. Gathering speed, the car pulled away from Max, who took out his Mauser pistol and fired two warning shots.

"Stop!"

The man in the car ignored him and sped up towards the main gate but just as he got close, two police cars appeared and skidded to a halt in front of his car, blocking the only way out.

Max caught up to them.

"I'm Max Hurlock on the Governor's Task Force and this man just murdered Mr. Warfield."

"You're crazy!" the man protested. "I didn't do anything. I was just looking for the police."

"Well this is your lucky day," said Max, "because you'll be seeing plenty of police where you're going."

Max turned to the police sergeant.

"Sergeant, if you will search this man, I believe you will find a freshly fired pistol and some fake whiskers."

"Is that so?" said the sergeant, patting the man down. "Well, here is a pistol. Looks like a .38." He sniffed the end of the barrel. "Smells like it's just been fired, too. Now let's see what's in those pockets. Why, did you ever? Here's a fake beard, just as you said."

"I don't know how that got there," said the man. "Someone must have planted that on me."

"Oh, really?" said Max. "And I suppose they planted that on you as well."

218

Max pointed to a thin streak of some shiny residue along each of the man's cheeks.

"What is that?" said the police sergeant. "Looks like glue."

"That," said Max, "is spirit gum. It's an adhesive used for affixing wigs, whiskers, false noses and the like for theatrical performances. The problem is that it requires a solvent to remove it completely, and this gentleman didn't have the time. I imagine he has a small bottle of the solvent in his automobile."

"You cops think you're so clever" snarled the man. "You should be arresting the land barons. They're the real criminals."

"If you'll bring this gentleman back to the house, I'll be glad to explain," said Max.

"And just what is this man's name then?"

"I don't know his name yet," Max admitted, "but I believe that his brother's name is Albert Nyborg."

The man looked at Max with daggers in his eyes. "How in the hell..."

One of the police pulled a wallet from the man's pocket and fished out the driver's license.

"Victor Nyborg, you are under arrest."

"Victor it is, then," said Max. "However, you probably know him better as the Invisible Man."

"The Invisible Man? Well," said the sergeant, "we'd better put some cuffs on you, my lad. Wouldn't want you to become invisible again, would we?"

Back at the house, the police cleared the crowd out of the gallery and brought the Invisible Man inside.

As Max and Allison entered, they were surprised to see Warfield sitting in an armchair in his undershirt and very much alive.

"That's the man!" he shouted hoarsely. "That's the man who attacked me!"

219

"Mr. Warfield, you're alive. What happened? I thought he shot you."

"He did; twice, but I told you I had made preparations."

"Preparations for being shot?" Allison asked.

Warfield chuckled. "I collect all sorts of art, you know, including old armor. Well, when firearms first came along, the old armor makers responded by making breastplates thicker and stronger to give more protection. As firearms improved, they had to give it up, but they left a lot of examples of their attempts."

"Armor?" said Max.

"This example here is one of the best." Warfield leaned over and picked up his shirt, but to everyone's surprise, it was backed by thick padding, and a steel breastplate with two round dents in it.

"What people forget is that the old muskets that penetrated armor were very big caliber, maybe .70 or so, but this plate will usually stop a .38, and it did. Of course, I didn't realize the impact of the thing. It pushed me off my chair and knocked the wind out of me. I could hardly talk at first, and I'll have a couple of pretty big bruises in the morning."

"We thought you were dying," said Max.

"No, just knocked about a bit."

The sergeant was scratching his head. "So what exactly happened?"

"Would you like to tell the good sergeant?" Max asked the Invisible Man. "I'm sure it's not every day he gets to investigate a real-life locked room murder."

"I want an attorney and I'm not talking to anybody," the man grumbled.

"Too bad. Well, then maybe I can fill in," said Max. "Mr. Victor Nyborg here is traveling around Florida murdering real estate people in revenge for the death of his brother who committed suicide in a fit of despondency over some bad local property investments. Mr. Nyborg has been committing these outrages in dramatic and electrifying ways to assure maximum publicity for his cause. He saw an opportunity to murder Mr. Warfield in a suitably spectacular and mysterious way when he found out about the gallery and the annual open house reception. He knew Warfield would be in the gallery with no guards and an unlocked door, so if he could get in and kill him, lock the only door behind him, then escape unnoticed, the effect would be sensational. He had read an article and seen photos, perhaps, that showed Mr. Warfield always wore a dark brown suit, had a grey beard and was bald, so he came up with an ingenious plan. Victor Nyborg shaved his head, then attended the reception wearing a dark brown suit with a reversible jacket that was a light tan on the reverse side. At that point, he was just a clean shaven bald man wearing a tan jacket."

The sergeant looked at the jacket Nyborg was wearing.

"By god, it is reversible at that. Tan on one side and dark brown on the other."

"So at the appropriate time," Max continued, "he slipped into the hallway bathroom, reversed his jacket to the dark brown side, pasted on the false whiskers, then casually walked to the gallery and let himself in. Anyone who saw him would assume he was Mr. Warfield. Remember, they didn't know Warfield was already in the gallery. So he entered, locked the door behind him, shot Mr. Warfield, tore off the whiskers, then turned the jacket back to the tan side while we were breaking down the door. The door swung inward, so he stood where the open door would shield him from view while everyone would rush in naturally focused on the body. Then, when there were enough people to cover him, he emerged from behind the door, mingled with the crowd, then slipped out as the clean shaven bald man that had been around earlier."

"That's right," Warfield added. "When he showed up in the doorway, I was so surprised by his appearance, I forgot to pick up my gun. Then he shot me and that's all I remember until Max burst through the door."

"So the effect of the plan," Max concluded, "was that witnesses would say they saw Mr. Warfield go into the gallery and lock the door. Then they would hear the shots and break the door down to find Warfield murdered without seeing anyone else enter or leave the gallery and presto, a classic murder in a locked room in full view of scores of witnesses. It would have been a masterpiece. The police would be baffled and the Invisible Man would have been triumphant once more. It was a clever plan and almost fooled me as well; by the time I figured out what happened, he was out the door, but Allison spotted him and raised the alarm."

"She sure did," said Warfield. "That young lady should be an opera singer." He turned to Allison. "But how did you know the man you saw was the killer?"

"That was simple," Allison said. "He was heading for the front door while everyone else was crowding into the gallery. Everyone else wanted to see what happened, but it was clear that he already knew and that he wanted to get far away from it."

Warfield shook his head. "Two detectives in one family. And Max, I owe you an apology. I underestimated this Invisible Man and almost paid with my life. I should have listened to you."

Max shrugged. "It all worked out in the end, but I thought you were going to point the gun at any stranger who showed up in your doorway?"

"I was," said Warfield, "but I was so startled to see someone who looked like me, I hesitated."

"Too bad *he* didn't," said Allison.

"Well, I think we need to take Mr. Nyborg here to a county jail cell," said the sergeant. "The higher ups can figure out the charging documents."

"I'll call the sheriff in St Augustine and see how he wants to proceed," said Max.

Warfield stood up. He winced at the pain from the bruises.

"My friends; the party is still on. There are plenty of drinks and plenty of food. Enjoy yourselves!"

Everyone cheered; everyone except the Invisible Man.

John Reisinger

Chapter 31
Seeing the Invisible Man

INVISIBLE MAN CAUGHT IN THE ACT
Quick thinking by detective duo saves the day

"DEAD MAN" ATTACKS LOCAL REAL ESTATE MOGUL
Nabbed by detective
Warfield party continues

LOCKED ROOM MURDER FOILED
Ingenious plot exposed
Police come in nick of time

INCREDIBLE SCENE AT WARFIELD ESTATE
An attempted "Locked Room Murder"

Max put the papers down and rubbed his temples. "And to think Glenn Curtiss wanted the case solved quietly."

They had just arrived back at the Alcazar in St Augustine late the night before and gone straight to bed. Now they were going to breakfast and picked up several newspapers at a nearby newsstand.

"Come on, Max. Why so glum? You caught the bad guy and saved a man's life. Not bad for a day's work," said Allison.

"It was considerably more than a day," Max replied. "Besides, I didn't save Warfield, his armor did."

Allison was having none of it. "You made him take that precaution by warning him in your previous visit; you rushed the killer by pounding on the door before he was ready, and you helped the police head him off. Most importantly, you were the one to keep the case alive when everyone else thought they had it solved. So stop the false modesty. It doesn't become you."

Max squeezed her hand.

"You always know how to burst my bubble when it needs it the most."

The desk clerk approached.

"Mr. Hurlock? There is a telephone call for you, sir. It's a Mr. Curtiss."

"Great. He's probably going to have them revoke my pilot's license."

"Well, they can't take Gypsy. She's paid for," said Allison.

"Hello, Max?" came the voice on the line. "I knew you could do it and I knew you'd run rings around the police. Max, you did me proud, and D.P. Davis can stop sleeping with a gun under his pillow."

"But I thought you wanted it done quietly," Max said.

"Bah! A case like this has sensation written all over it. You might as well try to keep a thunderstorm quiet. This will be all over the country, and the more people talk about it, the more they'll know that Florida is open for business with no distractions."

"But I never meant to embarrass the local police."

"Oh, don't worry about that," Curtiss chuckled. "The governor is all ready to hold a press conference at noon today patting himself on the back for appointing the task force. Since you were an informal member, he'll be able to spread the glory like manure on a cornfield. Atley will get the credit for coordinating the various police jurisdictions as well as eliminating the suspects, and every other department in the state will end up taking a bow for something or other."

"Success has a thousand fathers, but failure is an orphan," said Max.

"Exactly, so enjoy what little glory will be left for you. I'll be up there tomorrow. Why don't we have dinner with D.P. and Allison?"

"That would be fine. I'll see you then."

"Well, you did it, Max," said Atley when Max arrived at the sheriff's office. "You were right all along. Carpellini was telling the truth. He just got tired of the Navy and moved to Florida. Sorry I doubted you, but I grabbed at Carpellini just like everyone else. It just goes to show you can't always eliminate a suspect just because he's dead."

Max and Atley were in the interview room away from the prying eyes and questions of the reporters who prowled the rest of the office.

"Hey. It's almost time for the governor's press conference. Let's get that radio in here."

The radio, an old Philco that looked as if it had been used as a football, was soon brought in to the interview room and turned on. After some fiddling with the dial, Atley came on a station.

"....from the Governor's Office. We now take you to our live broadcast from Tallahassee. Please stand by for Governor Martin."

John Reisinger

There was more static and radio squeals, then the voice of the governor came through.

"My fellow Floridians, only a few days ago, out of concern for the safety of our citizens, I established a task force to coordinate law enforcement efforts to bring the so called Invisible Man to justice and to stop a series of cold blooded murders without precedent in our fair state. This task force consisted of the most distinguished names in professional law enforcement in the state, along with criminal specialists from Florida and beyond."

"That's you, Max," said Atley.

"I am pleased to formally announce that the task force has already borne fruit. Just yesterday, as a result of sound police work and dogged determination of all these people working as a team, the Invisible Man was apprehended in the very midst of his latest would-be crime. The actual arrest was made by local police under the direction of an associate member of the task force using data gathered by the entire team. As a result of the fine job done by the task force, a killer has been stopped in his tracks and the citizens of Florida are safer than they were just a few days ago. The man arrested is Victor Nyborg, from Vermont. I will be making further announcements when more details are available, but for now, sleep well, Floridians. Your state is in good hands."

"And now a word from Cliquot Club Ginger Ale..."

Atley snapped off the radio. "Can you beat that? He never even mentioned your name, Max."

"That's politics, Roy G.," said Max. "Look, I don't have to run for office. The governor needs the publicity a lot more than I do."

"Yeah, maybe, but I know the real story, Max, and so do plenty of others."

Knowing they were leaving soon for home, Max and Allison made another trip to Davis shores that afternoon and to Bubba and Nancy.

"Dang! Knew you could do it Max," said Bubba. "Honey, didn't I tell you Max could do it?"

"Yes, you did," Nancy agreed.

"Well, look," said Max. "We're heading back tomorrow, so we just wanted to say good bye and wish you luck down here. By the way, you were right about the killer getting careless and making his plans more complicated. That's what did him in."

"I thought so," said Bubba. "Guess I learned some law enforcement in that hall monitor job after all."

"I wouldn't go that far," Max laughed, "but you did learn. I think you'll do fine in Florida."

Bubba looked serious for once. "Max, the way I figure it, Florida is a place folks can start over, no matter what they did where they came from. Nancy and me, well, we're going to make a new life. We're gonna have a baby come fall. Just think; another Bubba!"

"Congratulations, Nancy," said Allison.

"Thanks. Say, maybe you and Max should think about it, too."

"Yes," said Allison. "Maybe we should."

They arrived back at the hotel around four. Allison headed up to the room while Max made arrangements' at the desk for check out the next day and for railroad tickets north. When he was finished, Max headed for the elevators and was surprised to see Allison talking with Julian DeKuyper. They were just finishing up, apparently, for Allison was holding out her hand.

"Well, goodbye, Julian. Best of luck to you."

Instead of shaking her hand, however, Julian bowed and kissed it. Allison smiled and stepped on the elevator. As the doors closed, Julian stood rooted on the spot, staring at where Allison had just been and wearing a look like a lovesick schoolboy. It was all too much for Max.

"Julian," said Max. DeKuyper turned around and smiled broadly.

"Ah, Max. I was just saying goodbye to Allison."

"So I noticed," said Max. "Julian, I'm curious. Why have you been hanging around Allison so much the past few weeks?"

"She's a charming woman, Max."

"Do tell. But she's a charming married woman."

DeKuyper looked shocked. "Max, really. I was just being hospitable."

"Nobody is that hospitable. What gives?"

"Oh, Max. I do hope you are not jealous in any way because you have no need to be. Allison has no romantic interest in anyone but you. I can tell these things. It's one of the reasons I find her so fascinating."

"You find another man's wife fascinating? What are you talking about?"

De Kuyper's smile faded. "I suppose it has looked unseemly at times. Max, the truth is that I had a wife myself, a wonderful woman very much like Allison. Her name was Pearl; she was exciting and fun to be around, and every day was a new adventure. Well, two years ago, she died of pneumonia, one of those freak things that just got out of hand. By the time they found it, there was nothing they could do. It was like the light went out of my life. I didn't know how I could go on. Finally, I moved to Florida to make a new start, and I'm doing all right, but occasionally, I'll run into a woman that reminds me of Pearl. When I do, I want to be around her, like a plant craving the sun. I have no designs on a woman like that, especially if she's married, I just need a little taste, a reminder of what I once had. I suppose it's hard to understand, but talking to Allison and sensing her love for you sort of, well, refreshes me. It reminds me that the qualities I once had in Pearl still exist, and maybe one day,..."

His voice trailed off.

Max felt embarrassed by his jealousy, and said a few encouraging words to Julian. Finally, he stepped towards the elevator.

"Good luck, Julian. You keep looking. She might be out there looking too."

Julian shook his hand with an unexpectedly strong grip. He didn't let go right away.

"Max, you have something in Allison that is rare and wonderful. Don't ever take her for granted."

"Don't worry, Julian. I won't."

He relaxed his grip and Max stepped on to the elevator. As the doors closed, DeKuyper was still standing there.

Back in the room, Allison was already starting to pack. Max said nothing about his meeting with DeKuyper, but Allison brought it up. "Max, I saw Julian on my way up and said goodbye."

Max didn't reply.

"He's such a nice man, but a little odd in some ways."

"Odd?"

"Well, when I left, he actually kissed my hand."

"And you consider that odd?" said Max.

"Not the kissing. It was what he said when he was doing it. He spoke very softly, almost as if he was talking to himself and said 'Goodbye, Pearl'. What do you suppose that was all about? It didn't mean anything to me."

"Maybe not," said Max, "but I'm sure it meant something to him."

In spite of his earlier refusal to talk, Victor Nyborg, it turned out, was only too glad to talk once he had a lawyer and access to the press. In a press conference later that day, radio listeners heard Victor Nyborg, against the advice of his attorney, read a prepared statement.

"My name is Victor Nyborg and I am from Vermont. My younger brother Albert came to Florida a year ago with a dream, a dream of a better life for himself and his wife. Encouraged and led on by Thomas Russo and others like him, Albert invested all his life savings in property whose value, he was promised, could only increase. Albert was a clerk; he wasn't a real estate professional, but Thomas Russo was. Thomas Russo knew the real value and the real prospects of the property he sold, so Albert took his advice."

Behind Victor Nyborg, a careful listener could easily make out the voice of his attorney making one last try. "Victor, please. This is not in your best interests. Leave any public statements for the trial."

Nyborg plowed ahead. "So Albert sunk all his life savings in property he soon found he couldn't resell. The monthly payments were taking what little income he had. He was sliding into bankruptcy and was about to become destitute. He contacted Thomas Russo for relief, but was ignored. He worked a second job and borrowed money to stay afloat, but in the end, he was doomed. Under the crushing pressure of the situation he found himself in, my brother finally snapped and took his own life. My brother was not to blame, since he relied on the word of the experts. No, the real villains were those who led him down the path to insolvency with promises of riches and those people needed to be brought to justice for hanging a person with his own dreams. I sought to give my brother that justice, even if posthumously."

As Nyborg finished his statement, reporters shouted questions at him.

"Is that why you killed all those men?"

"How many did you plan to kill altogether?"

"Do you have anything to say to the families of your victims?"

"How do you feel?"

But Nyborg's attorney, looking exasperated, hustled him back to his cell before he could answer.

Max, listening back at the hotel with Allison, snapped off the radio.

"That was about as close to a full confession that you're likely to get," Allison observed.

Max nodded. "Yes. He was so anxious to get his story out that he threw caution to the winds. They won't have much trouble getting a conviction now, I expect."

Allison agreed. "Seeing as how he was caught in the act of attempting yet another murder, I don't think convicting him would be a big problem in any event. Still, a *mea culpa* is always nice in these situations."

"Yes, it makes it less likely I'll have to come back to testify. I don't think the Florida authorities would want to showcase me in court anyway."

"No kidding; to hear the authorities tell it, you were just tagging along. Well, it'll be nice to get back. I already made an appointment with Doctor Lewis up in Easton to see how the Max Jr project is going."

"Are you worried?" Max asked.

"Well, you never know. There are some people who can't have children."

"Yeah, well, there are a lot who *shouldn't* have them, too, and unfortunately they are seldom the same people. But you'll be fine. If it's any compensation, I sometimes worry about whether I can be a father."

"Aren't we a pair? Well, everyone is insecure about something, I guess."

"I guess. We have to meet Curtiss and D.P. Davis for dinner in a couple of hours."

"Mmmmm. Two hours alone in a luxurious bedroom. Whatever shall we do?"

Max latched the door.

The dining room at the Alcazar seemed even brighter and more luxurious than ever that night. Diners chatted at the tables while candles flickered and waiters rushed to the kitchen and emerged with trays of delicacies. Glenn Curtiss and his wife sat at a table with Max, Allison, and D.P. Davis.

"Where is your wife, D.P. ? I wanted to meet her," said Allison.

"Oh," said D.P., "Elizabeth was a debutant and the Gasparilla Queen of 1925, so she still gets involved in these charity binge; she had one tonight and couldn't get out of it. Besides, she's mad at me for something or other."

Max thought it best to change the subject, so he turned to Curtiss.

"So I guess it's full speed ahead with your developments now."

Curtiss smiled. "It was always full speed ahead. Full speed ahead is what I've been doing all my life. The difference is that now, maybe the public will follow. I have you to thank, Max. The governor feels the same way."

"Really? You'd never know it."

"He's a politician, and he won't be getting any votes from Maryland, so he has to play up the Florida angle. He called me today, as a matter of fact. He wanted me to tell you that he knows what you did for the state and he's grateful. Oh, and he asked for your address in St Michaels."

"Oh? Is he planning on dropping by?" said Max.

"I haven't got a thing to wear," said Allison. "We get so few gubernatorial visits."

"No, I think he just wants to send you something."

"Well, Glenn, it wasn't easy, but it seems to have worked out," said Max over a prime rib. "I had some anxious moments, but I'm glad you thought of me and got me down here."

"I'm glad you both came down," said Curtiss. "Allison, too."

Max nodded towards Allison. "I couldn't have done it without her."

"No, you probably couldn't have. I know about engines, Max. I've built and tested hundreds of them. One thing I learned early was that for an engine to run properly, all the parts have to work together. If you have one bad part, even a minor one, it throws everything off. You and Allison are two parts of a very smoothly functioning engine, and together, there's no place that engine cannot take you."

Back in their room, Max and Allison looked out over the lights of St Augustine. Faint yellow mists of reflected humidity formed halos around the street lamps. Max put his arm around her shoulder and pulled her close to him.

"Well, tomorrow we climb aboard the Florida East Coast Railroad to begin the trip back to St Michaels. Will you miss St Augustine?"

"I'll miss the warmth and the lush beauty of Florida, and we've met some nice people, but it will be nice to get back. St Michaels is home."

"And nobody is killing anyone, at least I hope not."

The next morning, they emerged from the elevator to walk to the waiting car. Max half expected to see Julian DeKuyper in the lobby, but he was nowhere to be found. Max felt oddly disappointed.

"Hi, lady!"

Allison looked down and saw Billy, her little cowboy-hatted nemesis looking up at her.

"Oh, hello Billy."

"We're going home today. Mommy got all sunburned."

"Oh...That's too bad, Billy. Did you have a good time?"

"I went in the ocean! There were these big waves, and lots of sand. I made a castle, but the waves came in and messed it up. I like Florida. Do you like Florida, lady?"

"Very much, Billy. And do you know what?"

"What?"

Allison squatted down until her eyes were level with Billy's.

"If I have a little boy of my own, I hope he's just like you."

Billy stared at her a moment, then turned and went running for his parents, who had just finished checking out.

"Well," she said to Max. "I guess I haven't lost my knack with children. I still send them running for the hills."

They walked out of the lobby past a knot of people standing waiting for cabs. As they passed, Allison heard a familiar small voice from somewhere in the crowd.

"I saw that lady again, Mommy. She's really nice. I like her."

Allison smiled. Maybe she wasn't so bad with children after all.

John Reisinger

Chapter 32
Back home

After the lush green vistas of Florida, St Michaels looked particularly bleak. Although it was almost April, the trees were still bare, the grass was brown, the farm fields were desolate except for some stubble, and an icy wind blew in off the bay, making the citizens clutch their coats tightly as they scurried about their daily business. Workboats went out to the oyster beds every morning and returned every night, sometimes with ice coating their decks.

Despite the newspaper articles praising the Florida Task Force and its "brilliant success" in tracking down and apprehending the Invisible Man, no one in St Michaels was fooled for a minute, especially with Isis Dalrymple acting as Max and Allison's informal publicity agent.

"It was good old fashioned detective work that did it," she would say. "The Hurlocks would make Philo Vance hang his head in shame. That Invisible Man character tried to be clever, but he didn't know what clever was. Now he's in jail."

Max called Chip Carswell and told him of his dinner with Bubba.

"Holy smokes, Max. You found him in another state? This is fantastic. My editor will be disappointed it wasn't a juicy foul play story, but I'm happy for old Bubba's sake. Hey, how about an exclusive interview about the Invisible Man case?"

"I'm keeping officially mum about it, but if you do an article about it, I'll be glad to tell all as long as I remain anonymous."
"Fair enough!"

When they first arrived home, Max and Allison found a large box waiting for them with a shipping label marked Tallahassee, Florida. Inside was a crate of fresh Florida oranges with a note.

Max: It was thanks to you that the investigation finally bore fruit, so I thought I'd return the favor. Thanks for everything,
John Martin, Governor

The next day, they received a large envelope postmarked Miami Springs, Florida. Inside was a bonus check from Glenn Curtiss, along with a framed photo of Curtiss standing next to a Curtiss Jenny. The inscription said

To Max Hurlock, a great detective and a great aviator, and Allison, the great lady who inspires him. Thanks again, Glenn Curtiss

Max looked at the picture, speechless. Finally, Allison broke the silence.
"Now don't stare a hole in it, Max. We want it to look its best when we place it in our trophy room."
The picture was hung in a place of honor next to the ceramic tiger from the Ellsworth Connelly case in New York, and under the Membership certificate in the Jekyll Island Club from the Dawkins poisoning case in Georgia, the knife from the Devil's Elbow lighthouse murder near Crisfield, and the bootlegger's

notebook from the Taylor-Bradwell case in New Jersey. On a side table, Max noticed Allison had placed the beans she had gotten from the Voodoo shop.

"We're getting our own little 'Black Museum' here," said Max. "Soon, we could sell tickets."

"Maybe we could add a picture of Bubba Henderson while we're at it," said Allison, picking up her purse. "Well, I'm off."

"You're going into town?" Max asked.

Allison nodded. "I'm stopping by to see if Knobby Miller has finished that bird I asked him to carve for me, and I have a doctor's appointment."

"Doctor? Oh, you mean the..."

"Yes."

Max grabbed her arm as she went to leave. She turned around and faced him.

"Look, Allison. I know we've made a big thing of this whole Max, Jr project and, well, I know we've each had some worries about whether we could...you know."

"I know."

He looked in her eyes. "Well, I just wanted you to remember, that whatever happens, I love you and nothing can change that. A baby won't change that and the lack of a baby won't either. Do you understand?"

"Of course," she whispered.

They embraced, and after a kiss, she was gone. Max watched the Model T disappear down the drive as it had so many times before, but this time, it was different. This time it meant their lives were about to change, one way or another.

Allison didn't return right away, and as the time passed, Max became uneasy. He wrote a report on the Invisible Man case so he would have a record, then, seeing Allison was still gone, worked in the barn for a while, cleaning and polishing Gypsy. Curtiss had given him some tips and tricks for dealing with a Jenny and Max had been anxious to try them. After a long while, Max cleaned his hands and sat on a barrel, looking at the airplane.

"It's funny," he said out loud, "but an airplane in the hanger is something you have complete control over. You can adjust; you can add to it; you can tune the engine; you can pretty much do what you want to plan for anything that might happen. But once you start flying, things happen that you didn't count on, things that can be dangerous. It's a sobering thought that you have even less control with people and with the course of your life. You just have to do the best you can and hope everything comes out all right."

Max sighed and went behind the barn to stack some firewood for a while. When he came back around and looked at the house, he saw the Model T was back. Allison had returned and he hadn't heard her. What was even more unsettling was that she had gone in the house when she arrived and hadn't called him or come looking for him. Why not? Was it bad news? Maybe she was looking for him inside and was about to come out.

Cautiously, Max approached the house. She wasn't calling for him. He would have heard that. Whatever she was doing, it didn't seem to require him. Max's heart sank. This could only mean bad news. How would he console her for such a bitter disappointment? She had been so happy when they had decided to start a family, and talked excitedly about Mussolini and dogsled drivers, and now this. What could he possibly say or do to make it better, to ease the pain?

He stood a minute longer. There was no sound from inside the house. If she was crying, he couldn't hear it yet. He took a deep breath and stepped inside the front door.

"Allison? Where are you?"

"I'm in the bedroom." Her voice was flat.

Like a man climbing the gallows, he climbed the stairs, noticing how ominous the creaking sounded.

The bedroom was empty.

"No. The other bedroom," he heard her say.

Max felt a rise in his throat . That was supposed to have been the nursery. He stepped into the doorway and saw Allison.

She was smiling and wearing her best evening gown, complete with necklace, and was holding a silver platter with a cake on it. On top of the cake, with its feet planted firmly in the chocolate icing was the miniature wooden bird Knobby Miller had carved; a perfectly detailed, graceful stork.

The End

Notes:

The D.P. Davis case

The story in this book is fiction, but it is based on a real life case; the mysterious death of real estate developer D.P. Davis in 1926. D.P. Davis was a Florida-born, larger than life character who developed and built the Davis Islands off of Tampa, and Davis Shores across from St. Augustine, as well as smaller projects. Just as depicted in the book, Davis Shores was an upscale planned development built on a former swamp. Davis Shores, however, was still under construction when it was caught in the depression of the real estate market in Florida in 1926, and many buyers found themselves unable to make the monthly payments on properties they had hoped to resell at a profit. Some of these unhappy investors grumbled about fraud or improper advertising, and things were getting shaky for Davis in 1926.

Just a year earlier, Davis had married Elizabeth Nelson, a local debutante and Gasparilla Queen of 1925. Their relationship was a stormy one and there were rumors of a divorce when Elizabeth went to England in 1926. In October of that year, Davis boarded the luxurious passenger liner Majestic to go to England himself. With him was an entourage of friends, including his ex-mistress, Lucille Zehring, her mother, Davis's attorney, and private detective Raymond Schindler. Exactly why these people were along and what Davis intended to do once he arrived are not known, but on the night of October 12, Davis fell from the porthole of his stateroom into the North Atlantic. His body was never found.

Rumors of a wild party in his stateroom swirled, along with gossip that he committed suicide because of his financial trouble, was murdered by an unhappy investor, was murdered by someone else, faked the death to escape the financial problems, or simply suffered an unfortunate accident. Contradictory testimony was inconclusive and the death was officially put down as an accident.

Today, but Davis Islands in Tampa and Davis Shores in St Augustine are thriving communities.

Chapter 2
Mussolini
After pushing aside King Victor Emmanuel III with a "March on Rome" in 1922, the Fascist leader Benito Mussolini became the head of the Italian government and began building his power to an absolute dictatorship. Allison was probably reading of several laws passed in 1926 expanding Mussolini's power and building a police state. Il Duce (The Leader) as he called himself lead Italy into a disastrous war of conquest in Africa and alliance with Hitler, including sending Italian troops to aid in the German invasion of Russia. Unlike the Germans, however, relatively few Italians seemed to share their leader's thirst for glory and conquest. Mussolini was expelled from power by members of his own government and the king in 1943. After a period of imprisonment, he was placed in charge of a new Fascist government and propped up by the Germans. But fortune again turned against him and he fled for Switzerland with his mistress and several loyalists. He was captured by communist partisans and shot.

Chapter 2
The Nome Diphtheria epidemic of 1925 and the Iditarod

It would be hard to imagine a town more isolated and inaccessible than Nome, Alaska in the winter of 1925. With few reliable roads and no working aircraft, no one could get to or from the town in the snow and subzero cold. So when a Diphtheria epidemic broke out, the situation soon became critical. Vaccine was available elsewhere, but how to get it to Nome? The answer was a team of volunteer dogsledders who pushed on through temperatures as low as -60F to cover the bleak snow fields between themselves and Nome.

The dogsledders saved the day and the demanding trip is commemorated every year in the famous Iditarod dogsled race.

Chapter 7
Glenn Curtiss

Max's admiration for Glenn Curtiss was well founded. Glenn Curtiss got his start designing and building motorcycle engines and for years held the land speed record of 136mph. A natural inventor and innovator, he got into aviation engines, then airplanes themselves. Curtiss worked with a group that included Alexander Graham Bell and soon had two flying machines making public flights. Although the Wright Brothers had already made the first flight, they kept their work closed to the public. Soon Curtiss was winning speed and distance records with his newly designed airplanes.

Curtiss's work was slowed by a series of lawsuits brought by the Wright Brothers, who feared copyright infringement and being overshadowed. Even so, Curtiss invented ailerons, retractable landing gear, naval aviation, the first airplane to cross the Atlantic, and numerous other innovations. Ironically, business considerations led to the merger of his company with one founded by the Wrights to form the Curtiss-Wright Company.

Curtiss moved to Florida and went into the development business around Miami Springs, but was still interested in aviation and still kept inventing and designing improvements.

Chapter 8
The Alcazar hotel
The Alcazar Hotel was an ornate and luxurious structure originally built by Henry Flagler when he was building the railroad and opening Florida up to development in the 1890s. The building in which Max and Allison stayed was opened as the Casa Monica, but renamed the Cordova when purchased by Henry Flagler. In 1902 the Cordova was connected with the nearby Alcazar (Now the Lightner Museum) and called the Alcazar Annex. A year later, the two hotels were jointly named the Alcazar until they were closed in 1932. The hotel was bought by the St John's County Commission for use as a courthouse and later sold to Kessler Enterprises of Orlando. In 1999, the renovated and restored portion in which Max and Allison stayed was reopened as the Casa Monica, its original name.

Chapter 11
The old fort in St Augustine

The old fort in St Augustine was called Fort Marion in the 1920s and was an inactive army post. After being transferred to the National Park Service, it was renamed the Castillo de San Marcos National Monument and is a busy tourist attraction. The fort is a classic star shaped construction and is built with coquina stone, which is relatively soft and porous, absorbing cannon balls without cracking, but leaking moisture into the fort.

Chapter 11
Davis Shores

Davis Shores got off to a slow start. Between the 1926 real estate bust and the death of D.P. Davis that same year, the ambitious development had only six houses, two apartments and a sales office. Even the opening of the Bridge of Lions couldn't increase sales, and it was only after World War II that economic growth spurred demand and led to Davis Shores finally expanding. Today, Davis Shores is a prosperous community with the original layout and many of the original buildings intact.

Chapter 17
The Zorayda Club (Villa Zorayda)

Built by Boston Millionaire Franklin Smith as a winter home in 1883, the Villa Zorayda in St Augustine has served as a private residence, night club/speakeasy, gambling establishment, and museum. The Zorayda was one of the first St Augustine buildings to feature Spanish. Moorish architecture and was furnished with Middle Eastern antiques, including an ancient rug taken from a pyramid. As depicted in the story, the Zorayda was a speakeasy and gaming parlor during most of the 1920s and was called the Zorayda Club. The Villa Zorayda, also known as the Zorayda Castle has been restored and is a now well-known tourist spot in the heart of St Augustine.

Suggested discussion questions for book clubs

1. How did the Florida real estate boom and bust of the 1920s affect the budding tourist industry?

2. What factors led to the "Tin Can Tourists?"

3. Discuss Max and Allison's unease about the uncertainties of starting a family. Are these doubts that most couples experience?

4. How did the impossible nature of the crimes enhance the story? How did you think the crimes were committed before Max explained?

5. Who did you think was the killer and why?

6. How does Allison display her independence?

7. Why does Max keep his theories a secret from the sheriff until near the end?

8. Do you think the crimes are plausible? Discuss.

9. The Max Hurlock stories often feature unexpected twists, such as the real reason for Jullian DeKuyper's interest in Allison. Can you think of others?

Other adventures of Max and Allison Hurlock

Death of a Flapper
How did the most popular girl in town and her ex-fiancée end up dead and half-dressed in her locked bedroom? A distraught parent begs Max Hurlock to find the truth, but another murder occurs and the suspicious local police arrest Max for the crime!

"...fun and interesting, crammed with tidbits of historical information that gives it flavor and captures 1922 and early years of the Roaring 20s with real gusto." Amazon Review

Death on a Golden Isle
Death crashes the party at an exclusive island club for millionaires when a member is poisoned at the club dance. All eyes turn to his new wife and she turns to Max Hurlock to crack the case. But how do you pry secrets out of the most powerful men in America?

"...a delightful visit to an era, long past, with suspicions, secrets and clues woven through summer mansions, the exclusive club, and into shadowy hunting grounds." Amazon Review

Death at the Lighthouse
It's lights out on the Chesapeake Bay when a lighthouse keeper is murdered. Was it local rumrunners, a jealous husband, or something even more sinister? Max and Allison Hurlock must get to the bottom of a case involving rumrunners, jealous husbands, watermen, spiritualists, a corrupt federal agent, and a certain well-known magician.

"Mark me down as a super-fan of John Reisinger. I predict that every lover of an exciting tale told well will agree." Anne Stinson, Tidewater Times Book Review

Death and the Blind Tiger
Ellsworth Connelly seemed to have it all. Operating out of his opulent bachelor townhome, Connelly left a string of jilted women, outraged husbands, and resentful business partners

in his wake. Was it any wonder he was found in his own parlor shot through the head? To exonerate his client, Max must deal with the local police, bootleggers, and assorted New York characters such as Duke Ellington, while Allison goes to the Algonquin round table to match wits with Dorothy Parker. Their only clue is a blindfolded ceramic tiger...sent by the dead man!

(Gold Medal winner in Mystery category- 2104 Global E-Book Awards)

"...takes the reader from the elegant homes of wealthy New Yorkers to the seamier side of a city living under Prohibition, and weaves the threads of that event through the story." Amazon Review

Death across the Chesapeake
The Hurlocks are back on Maryland's sleepy Eastern Shore to settle down to a quiet life after years of solving murders. But when a local stockbroker is killed in his locked office in a building owned by the wealthy and eccentric Stilwells, the Easton police know they have a delicate situation on their hands, and turn to Max and Allison for help. Several unhappy investors, a soon-to-be ex-wife, and a disappointed lady friend of the victim all have motives, and there seems to be some connection to the Stilwells themselves and their mysterious and well-guarded waterfront estate, Casa Leone. Max tries to put the pieces together, while Allison helps the mayor fend off the sensation-seeking press. The pressure mounts, but no one can say who killed the stockbroker, or even how he did it.
Add to the mix a man from Allison's past, an unlikely New York art dealer with a passion for mysteries, some ravenous reporters, a steel walk-in safe that seems to hold nothing of value, a book found at the crime scene that shouldn't be there, and a small, unexplained pile of plaster dust, and it soon becomes clear that Max's retirement from detective work was premature.

Books by John Reisinger

The Max Hurlock Roaring 20s Mysteries
Death of a Flapper
Death on a Golden Isle
Death at the Lighthouse
Death and the Blind Tiger
Death in Unlikely Places
Death across the Chesapeake

Historical novels
Flanagan and the Crown of Mexico
Nassau
Evasive Action
The Confessions of Gonzalo Guererro

Biography
Master Detective: The Life and Crimes of Ellis Parker, America's Real-life Sherlock Holmes

Children's
The Duckworth Chronicles
The Duckworth Papers
The Duckworth Dossier
Duckworth Redux

www.johnreisinger.com

John Reisinger

About the author

John Reisinger lives on Maryland's Eastern Shore, and is the author of Master Detective, the true story of detective Ellis Parker and his controversial involvement in the Lindbergh kidnapping investigation.

He also writes the Max Hurlock Roaring 20s Mysteries, based on real crimes of that era, as well as of several historical novels, including Nassau, Evasive Action, Flanagan and the Crown of Mexico, and The Confessions of Gonzalo Guererro.

John has appeared as a panelist or solo presenter at Deadly Ink, Malice Domestic, New England Crime Bake and Bouchercon conferences. Several of his presentations have been broadcast on local television and radio. John has also appeared on the TV series Mysteries at the Museum in a segment based on Master Detective.

His website is http://www.johnreisinger.com, and his blog is http://johnreisinger/wordpress.com

www.ingramcontent.com/pod-product-compliance
Lightning Source LLC
Chambersburg PA
CBHW030157200626
46812CB00017B/2343